Music of Her Heart

Stones Creek
Ladies of Sanctuary House 2

Sophie Dawson

May your life be a story in faithful living.

DEDICATION

TO my granddaughter. I love you.

Acknowledgements

Whenever I come to acknowledging those who helped with one of my books, I have a difficult time choosing. How does one give thanks and honor to all who took the journey of creation with me? I go over in my mind all those involved and try to think of those whom I haven't mentioned in the past. This time I'm going to acknowledge my dedicated team of editors and beta readers. They enthusiastically take my draft and pick it apart to find the flaws so I can make it better. They find the typos, poor grammar, and punctuation marking up the file with red ink. And so, I honor Carolyn, Joy, Linda, Ruth, Cindy, and Angie. Thank you so very much.

Disclaimer

This is a work of fiction. Most of the places within the story are fictitious, but some are real. You will most likely recognize those which are. Those you don't are made up by me. The people, unless you recognize the name of a real historical person, are not real. They, too, have been created by me or by my friend and author George McVey. This is true of Nugget Nate and Penny Ryder, who may or may not show up in this book. Even if real historical people are mentioned, their lives may or may not adhere strictly to documented historical reference. In other words, what they do or say has little bearing in fact and they probably didn't do or say it. This is a fictional story after all.

All Scripture is quoted from the World English Bible.

DESCRIPTION

RED Dickerson is shocked to see a young woman running through the woods in the freezing rain. He'd gone to the far end of Hawk's Wing Ranch to think after his engagement was broken by the woman he planned to marry. Recognizing her as Gema Volkovichna, one of the women from Sanctuary House, he spurs his horse to go after her. Finding she's escaped after being kidnapped by the infamous King Gang, he vows to keep her safe.

Gema Volkovichna is one of the newest women to come to Sanctuary House in Stones Creek, Colorado. She came to find work and possibly a husband. When a spring blizzard forces them to spend three days alone in a line shack, there's only one conclusion. She and Red must marry to salvage her reputation.

Can Gema and Red learn to be husband and wife? Will love grow from this forced marriage? Will the King Gang return to reclaim what they lost? Can Red and Gema learn to dance together to the MUSIC of HER HEART?

Sophie Dawson

CHARACTER LIST
MUSIC OF HER HEART

With the growth of Stones Creek and the many people who live there, I've decided a list of the main characters might be of interest and beneficial to the reader. Only the major characters are listed. This list includes those who appear in the Stones Creek Series and first book of Stones Creek Ladies of Sanctuary House Series. Children's ages reflect their age at the end of the book.

Sanctuary House Ladies and their children.

Gema Volkovichna

Blanche Basking

    Oswald Basking (Ozzie) - Blanche's son (13)

    William Basking (Will) - Blanche's son (11)

    Nancy Basking - Blanche's daughter (8)

    John Basking - Blanche's son (6)

Laura Duffle -Engaged to Hank Johnson

    Edward Duffle (Eddie) - Laura's son (9)

    Mark Duffle - Laura's son (7)

Ruth Naylor

    Kathryn Naylor - Ruth's daughter (12)

Cora Sepal

    Susan Sepal - Cora's daughter (3)

Libby Trembly

    Jack Tanner - Foster son to Libby (18 months)

Arleta Tanner - Foster daughter to Libby (18 months)

Other Main Characters

Reddington Dickerson (Red) - Foreman of Hawk's Wing Ranch

Hawk Conner - Owner Hawk's Wing Ranch

Alberto Valdez - Head wrangler on Hawk's Wing Ranch

Juanita Valdez - Housekeeper on Hawk's Wing Ranch Alberto's wife

Hank Johnson - Barber

Noah Preston - Preacher, Gunsmith

Flora Potter

Sally Rife

 Nina - Sally's daughter (3)

Ada (14)

Boone (12)

Mae (10)

Tadpole (8)

Stones Creek residents

Eli Steele - Doctor in Stones Creek

Leah Steele - Wife to Eli

Lincoln Pierce (Linc) - Foreman of Chasing R Ranch

Elenora Pierce (Norie) - Linc's wife, daughter of Wes Chase, owner of Chasing R Ranch

Wesley Chase (Wes) - Owner of Chasing R Ranch,

Norie's father

    Ben Cutler - Owner of Cutler's General Store

    Sara Cutler - Ben's wife

        Seth Cutler - Son of Ben and Sara (11)

        Abigail Cutler (Abby) - Daughter of Ben and Sara (9)

        Clayton Cutler - Son of Ben and Sara (3)

    Newt Riverby - Sheriff

    Myra Riverby - Sheriff Newt's wife

        Troy Hope - Myra's son (5)

    McIlroy - Blacksmith

    Chloe McIlroy - Blacksmith's wife

        Duncan Ashburn (Dunc) - Chloe's Son (14)

        Penelope Ashburn (Lil-Pen) - Chloe's daughter (5)

    Thomas Wilson - Ex-slave

    Almeda Wilson - Ex-slave, Thomas's wife

    Spike Hunter - Head wrangler on Chasing R Ranch

    Doris Hunter - Housekeeper on Chasing R Ranch, Spike's wife

    Vernie Preston - Noah Preston's wife

    Nugget Nate Ryder - Uncle of Ben Cutler

    Penny Ryder - Nate's wife

    Garfield Steele - Eli's father

    Chalmers Jehosaphat Ritter (CJ) - Banker

    Arty Massot - Carpenter

    Forsyth Franklin Fredrick Farnsworth the Fourth (Four) - Lawyer

CHAPTER ONE

Stones Creek, Colorado
March 1869

ALL SHE could hear was the blood pounding in her ears and the ragged intake and exhale of air as she ran. Gema Volkovichna didn't look back. She just ran. She had to get away. That woman, Flora, had placed herself in danger for her. Gema wasn't going to allow that to be wasted.

She hadn't a clue where she was going, just away. Away from the small cave that the group of outlaws was using as their hideout. Away from certain rape and abuse.

Terror drove Gema on. She tripped, nearly falling. She wished the clouds would break so she could see the sun. She had no idea what direction she was running. Was she heading toward Stones Creek or away? Were the trees thinning? If she left the cover of the forest would they find her? Stones Creek was near where the land sloped up from plains to forested hills. Just past the edge of town, the woods began.

If only she could get back to Stones Creek. Then she'd be safe. Or would she? She'd been kidnapped right from the street in the middle of the day. Or rather the alley behind the hotel where she worked as a maid.

Gema had left the hotel by the back door to go have her midday meal at Sanctuary House where she lived. She hadn't been in the Colorado town long. Only since January. It was now late-March.

As she walked behind the hotel, Gema was grabbed from behind and flung over the back of a horse. Whoever was holding her across the saddle kicked the horse into a gallop before she could even try to scream. The saddle horn dug into her hip. It wasn't long before the pins of her hat were lost and it fell to the ground. Gema hadn't a clue how far they traveled. She might have even fainted for a while.

When the horse was brought to a halt, Gema was dumped to the ground. Her blonde hair was streaming around her face and shoulders, the pins having long past lost their grip on the blonde strands. She looked up from her crouch on the ground and saw men leering down at her. Grins that spoke of their intent stole her breath.

"Please, let me go." Gema knew they wouldn't understand her words. She'd spoken in her native Russian. Her fear made the use of English impossible.

"Well, girly, I ain't got no clue abouts what you're sayin', an' I don't rightly care. You're a fine lookin' piece, I must say. Nice 'n trim. You'll do us mighty fine." The man was dirty and missing several teeth. His beat-up cap sat low over his forehead. Another man stood next to him. Licking his lips. Two more were securing the horses to brush nearby.

Gema looked around, frantically searching for a place to run. She backed up. A rock cliff rose behind, stopping her retreat. What was she going to do? *Lord, help me. Please don't let them…* She couldn't even think the words.

"What have you done now?" Gema turned toward the sound of a woman's voice. A large boned woman in ratty clothing stood with her hands on her hips in the opening to a dark cave.

"We done brought us another woman. She'll take up what Prue used to do. Maybe some of Roda's tasks too, now that they's both dead," the man said.

Another woman came to stand behind the first. "No, Ornan. You have to take her back. They'll come after us for sure. What are we gonna do iffen we have to hightail it outta here? We've still got sick young'uns."

More faces began appearing behind the women. Several children and young teens. All were thin, dressed in ragged garments, and several had faces covered in a red rash. Gema knew what that was. She'd been ill for nearly three weeks. Measles. The epidemic swept through Stones Creek beginning in late February. Several adults and children, including a woman living in Sanctuary House, died. The town was still recovering from the losses.

"Don't rightly care just now. I got me a new woman, and I'm fixin' on trying her out." The man, Ornan, took a step toward Gema.

"Nyet." Gema jumped up and began running. He caught her within four steps. She began swinging her fists, clipping him on the jaw.

Ornan smacked her across the cheek. "You'll learn to do as you're told."

"Ornan," the woman said. She strode to where they stood and jerked his hand from Gema's arm. "Can't you see she's scared to death? She might not even be able to understand what you say. She's speakin' some foreign language. If you take her now, she'll not accept her lot. She'll fight you, and you'll never be able to turn your back on her.

"Remember Edna? You all took her too soon, and she nearly killed Phil over there." She pointed at another man. There was a jagged scar running down his face. "She stabbed Fred, too. Then, you all beat her and left her. Fat lot of good it did you to grab her and use her right away."

Ornan studied Gema. She flinched back when he reached out. "You gotta point." He looked at the other men. "How about we wait a couple of days. Three at most. Get her used to being here. Then, we'll make sure she understands her place real well."

There were grumbles, but the men were nodding as they did so.

Ornan grabbed Gema's arm again and jerked her to him. He landed a sour-breathed kiss on her mouth, then shoved her toward the woman. "That's just a sweet taste for your pleasure. I'll get mine later." He looked at the woman who stared back at him. "Take her into the cave. We men got us some planning to do." He turned and walked back to the men. They moved to a grouping of logs set around a fire pit.

"Come." The woman motioned to Gema who glanced back at the men, then followed her into the cave.

The space was large enough not to be crowded. There were three fire pits. Pallets were scattered around with blankets. A few had pillows. Saddle bags, food, and other supplies were in piles. There was a water barrel near the entrance. Nothing was clean or efficiently arranged. And the place smelled. Urine, feces, and vomit fought for dominance.

From the dim light of the fires, Gema could see a couple of children lying on pallets. The ones who had come to the cave opening retreated to lie down on others.

"I'm Flora," the woman said. "What's your name? Can you understand me?"

"Gema. I, Gema." The words were said barely above a whisper. She couldn't force more strength into them.

"Come and sit." Flora led her to a log near the fire. She went to the water barrel and dipped the ladle in, then brought it to Gema. "Drink."

Gema obeyed the command.

"Where'd they steal you from?"

"Stones Creek."

Flora swore. "Them idiots. They had to go to a town that has a sheriff who knows what he's doin'." She began pacing.

Another woman approached and held out a piece of dried meat and a tin cup with beans. Gema took them and spooned some beans into her mouth. They were tasteless, but she knew she had to eat.

"I'm Sally." She placed a cup of coffee next to Gema. She moved away and crouched down on the other side of the fire.

Someone started coughing. Sally moved to a pallet and picked up a small child whose long hair seemed to indicate it was a girl. When she came back to the fire, Gema could see that the little one had the measles. She was small and thin, with a dirty face covered in a red rash. Her eyes were swollen and watery.

Another child, a boy somewhat older came over and sat next to Sally. He leaned against her. He looked to be about eight. In the firelight, Gema couldn't tell whether he was coming down with the measles or recovering. The rash on his face was lighter than on the girl's.

Flora paced back and stood in front of Gema. "You're going to leave. I'm not sure how, but you aren't staying here. I'm not going to be party to another woman's abuse by the likes of these men.

"When Lloyd was leader, he put a stop to the kidnappings. He's dead. Ornan started them up again." She looked over Gema's shoulder, focusing on the wall behind her. "Chloe got out. I thought she'd died back in Minnesota where we abandoned her. I felt just awful when Buster King did that. She was so close to giving birth." Flora turned her gaze onto Gema again. "I didn't know she was still alive until I heard Buster say she was living in Stones Creek. That give me hope. Hope that maybe someday I can get out."

Flora squatted down and looked Gema in the eye. "I'm gonna do whatever it takes to give you the chance to get outta here. You're gonna take it, you hear? You're gonna grab the chance and run as fast and far as you can. Don't think about any of us. We know what to do. How to live."

Sally came over and placed a hand on Flora's shoulder. "What are you gonna do?"

Flora looked up. "What do you think? I'm gonna give

them a distraction so Gema, here, can get away."

Gema found her voice, words in English. "What kind distraction?"

"Only two things will draw their attention, and the first will just point them back to you. So I'll get 'em good and drunk." Flora stood and marched over to a pile of supplies and pulled out several jugs. She came back, looked at Gema, then Sally. "You be sure to get her out of here."

~~~~~

Red Dickerson rode Ralph up the hill into the forest. He'd been on the far end of the ranch for several weeks, ever since his betrothal to Laura Duffle had ended. The owner, Hawk Connor, had given him permission to come up to the line shack and look for stray cows and calves even though he was the foreman of Hawk's Wing Ranch.

He'd also tasked Red with keeping an eye out for the gang of outlaws who were terrorizing the region. The leader, Buster King, and his brother had been captured late last year when they attempted to kidnap one of the House Ladies from the café where she worked. Since then, the rest of the gang had killed a settler and burned the homestead and barn. So far, they'd proven elusive. This remote area had several caves and plenty of water from the streams that ran down from the mountains.

Red was living in the shack and riding the hills and plains daily. He was doing a lot of thinking too. He'd messed up with Laura, and she'd given him the mitten. He wasn't that upset as they'd truly only been friends.

What bothered him more was that he now had to figure out where and how to find another woman he could be interested in enough to marry. He'd already eliminated each of the women of Sanctuary House.

Last summer eight women and their children had come to Stones Creek to live in the house Nugget Nate Ryder, the millionaire mountain man, had built. He had a mission for women in need back in Iowa called Sanctuary Place. Red had heard the stories of Nate having Callings from God to go to specific places. There, he found women who had fallen into hard times of their own making or that were thrust upon them. They were supported and given schooling, training, and especially the message that God so loved them that He gave His only Son for them.

With the dire shortage of women in the West, Nate built Sanctuary House so the women of his mission could move to Stones Creek with the possibility of finding husbands. To safeguard the women and their children, Nate gave four town leaders the obligation of approving each man before he could court one of the women. Only three of the original women were still unmarried.

In January, two more Ladies had come. Libby Trembly and Gema Volko-something. Neither of them had children, which was appealing, but Red had been involved with courting Laura at the time. Libby had a sadness about her that Red didn't think he'd ever be able to breach. Gema was only twenty. At thirty-four, Red thought she was too young for him.

Well, maybe if another batch of women came this summer, he'd find one he wanted to court. He'd be sure to watch his attitude and tongue next time.

Rain had begun falling about a half an hour before,

and with the temperature dropping, it was beginning to turn into sleet. Red was thankful he'd bought one of the new hats Ben Cutler w as selling in his store. It was made by an eastern company called Stetson. Wide-brimmed and made of felted fur, the hat was expensive but looked as though it would last him a lifetime. It kept the sun out of his eyes and was now keeping the rain and sleet from slipping past his collar and down his back.

A flash of white appeared between the trees. Not the white you'd see on a cow. No, it was more the white of a shirt.

Red kicked his horse to speed him up. He studied the area as he approached, slowing Ralph to a walk. Hawk had warned him not to try to take on the outlaws. All he was going to do was scout and see if he could tell where their hideout might be.

The white darted between trees again. Yellow trailed behind. Not yellow cloth, blonde hair. Long blonde hair. Whoever it was had long hair and was probably a woman. Red kicked Ralph into a trot. A woman out here in the rain and sleet was in danger whether she was part of the outlaw gang or not.

As Red moved closer, he got a better glimpse of the woman. His jaw dropped, and he almost did the same to the reins. That was Gema Volko-something. Her Russian name always escaped him, not that he could pronounce it anyway. What was she doing this far from Stones Creek? Without a coat. The day had started off warm for late March, but the weather was fickle, and the temperature was dropping fast.

He saw Gema glance behind her and scream. She ran even faster, dodging between the trees. Red called her name, hoping she'd recognize his voice. She just kept running.

Then, she went down, falling into a small stream that cut its way down the hillside. Red caught up just as she was trying to get up. Her brown skirts were soaked, making it difficult for her to rise.

Red jumped off Ralph and ran to her, pulling her from the stream. Gema screamed and fought him, wind milling her arms, trying to hit him with her fists. He grabbed her hands, bringing her to his chest. He wrapped his arm around her, hoping to stop her struggles.

"Shh, Gema, it's Red Dickerson. You're safe with me. Shh." He kept up what he hoped were comforting words and sounds. He didn't know if she was understanding him in her panic. Finally, she stopped and looked up at him. Recognition seeped into her being. Gema laid her head on his chest and began to cry. She was trembling. Red didn't know whether it was from the cold and wet, or panic. He did know he had to get her out of the rain and into warm, dry clothing.

"Come, let's get away from here. When you're warm and dry, you can tell me why you're way out here." He led her over to Ralph. "Stand here while I mount. Then, I'll lift you up." He hugged her once before letting her go. "You're safe with me."

Red mounted, then reached down to lift her onto the saddle in front of him. There was no way, in her condition, that she could hold on to his waist or the back of the saddle. She was shaking too hard. By placing her in front, he could tuck her into his coat, sharing his warmth with her.

Soon, he had her settled against him, knowing she was as secure and protected as he could provide. "Hup," he said. Ralph began walking and Red turned the horse toward the line shack.

CHAPTER TWO

GEMA WAS trembling even more when they arrived at the line shack. Red dismounted, then lifted her off Ralph and carried her into the shack. Placing her on her feet next to the small stove, he quickly stirred the coals and added more wood. She just stood looking at him with wide frightened eyes.

Red looked at his laundry hanging to dry on lines strung across the room. One thing his courting of Laura had taught him was how to do laundry. Everything was dry so he pulled all the items off the line. Piling them on the table, he said, "Gema, I'm going to go tend Ralph. He needs to be taken into the lean-to, brushed, fed, and watered.

"See these clothes here. You get out of your wet things and into these. They aren't what you're used to wearing, but they are dry. It will help you warm up. We need to get you dry."

Gema looked at him and gave a slight nod. When he turned to leave, she grabbed his arm. "Don't leave me."

Red took Gema's hands. "I'm not leaving you. I'm just

going to put Ralph in the lean-to and settle him. It's attached to the back of the shack. You'll be able to hear me in there. Milly the donkey is in there, too. You change while I'm gone. Then, we'll make some coffee and food and try to get warm." Red touched her cheek. "You're safe here. No one but I will come in. I won't leave you. Get changed now."

She nodded. Red touched a finger to her cheek, then left to tend to the horse and donkey as quickly as possible. He'd bed them down now. He didn't think Gema would allow him to leave again once he got back.

When he was finished in the lean-to, Red took note of the weather. The sleet had changed to snow, and it was coming down in large wet flakes. Just her being here was going to damage her reputation. There was no way he could take her to Hawk's Wing Ranch homestead this evening. Not in this weather. He prayed it didn't turn into a blizzard. That would snow them in for who knew how long.

Red didn't want to think of the consequences of them being together overnight, let alone several days.

Red opened the door, slipped in and immediately turned toward the door. He shut it and lowered the wooden bar into place. His rifle went into the rack above. Turning around, the sight stopped him cold.

Gema stood with her bodice open and halfway down her arms. The fabric was sticking to her skin, and she was trying to pull it over her hands. He could see her shivering. Her fingers kept slipping off the fabric. She was concentrating on her task.

Red swallowed. Just what he needed: to help her

undress. "Miss Gema?"

She gave a little shriek and stumbled back. Red crossed the small room and caught her before she fell against the hot stove.

"I cannot undress. Fingers not work." Gema turned defeated eyes to him. They tore at his heart. He knew she had to be in shock and needed to get out of those wet things.

"Can I help? I don't want to do anything to scare you or hurt you."

Gema didn't answer. She simply held an arm up to him. Red swallowed again. So far, she was still covered fairly well. Nothing was revealed underneath but a white embroidered shirt. It was short sleeved but with buttons all the way up the front to a square neckline near her throat.

Part of her difficulty was that she'd forgotten to unbutton the cuffs. "Look here, Gema. You'll do better if you unfasten these little round things. What are they called?" He grinned just a little at her. Maybe teasing her a bit would help.

"Knopka."

"What?"

"Button." Her accent made the word sound like 'booton.'

"No, this is my boot on my foot." Red lifted his boot and twirled his foot around. Mud dripped off the leather, plopping on the floor. "Now, I made a mess. Comes with the weather."

While he was chattering, Red slipped first one, then the other sleeve off. The white bodice most likely would never be truly white again. It was stained and muddy from her fall into the stream. He set it on the chair.

He looked over her brown wool skirt. It hung in a sodden mass around her legs. He figured there would be a couple of petticoats, at least, underneath, soaked by her fall into the stream. That she hadn't moved from the spot he had placed her told him they probably weighed her down.

She fumbled at the side at the waistband, trying to unbutton it. Failing she looked up with pleading eyes. "Please?"

There was no help for it. He'd have to touch her waist to release the skirt. At least she wasn't wearing any sort of hoop or crinoline. Her skirts hung too close to her body.

Gema was shaking so hard he knew she had to be freezing. He needed to get her out of these things and into his clothes quickly. He thought he could hear her teeth chattering. Red released the button and began trying to push the skirt down.

"Nyet." She pushed his hands away.

"Gema, you need to let me help you get the skirt off."

"No, not down. Up. Over head."

"What?" Her accent was thicker than he remembered.

"Skirt, up, over head. Down no work."

Red examined the waist opening. She was right. There was no way the skirt would go down over the bulk of the petticoats. He bent and grabbed the hem, lifting it high. The waistband of the skirt stayed at her middle, with only the front of the skirt above her head. There was so much fabric it trailed down with the back hem still reaching the floor.

He began trying to gather more of the skirt into his hands, still holding them above her head. As he got a hold of one section of hem, another slipped out of his fingers. How in the world did a woman dress or undress herself with all this cloth? And there were more layers underneath.

A giggle came from within the bundle he was producing as he worked more fabric into his hands. "You make harder than is." Gema's hands appeared from under the waistband. She grabbed it and pulled the skirt up, over her head. When she let go, it fell to the floor with a slopping sound. Droplets of water splashed.

Red stepped back, then scooped up the skirt and laid it over the back of the chair. When he looked at her, Gema was pulling the drawstring tie of her petticoat open. It too was soaking wet with mud stains rising from the hem. As she drew the petticoat up, he helped her work it over her head. The dirty white fabric was leaving stains on the white of the shirt.

There was at least one more petticoat. She began untying the string as he set the first one aside. The petticoat began rising, and Red became more uneasy. What did she have on under this? Or not have on? He didn't know much about women's underpinnings, but somewhere there would be skin. Skin he wasn't supposed to see.

He squeezed his eyes shut and helped get the sodden garment off. Turning to the chair, he opened them a crack so he wouldn't either drop it on the floor or stumble into the chair or table.

Red turned to face her again and aimed his narrowed gaze at her lower legs. Another petticoat. His embarrassment would wait a little longer.

This one fell to the floor as he watched. Gema's boots and stockings came into view. Raising his gaze slowly, ready to shut his eyes if skin began to show, he breathed a sigh of relief when the hem of some white garment appeared.

When he looked up, Gema was trying to unbutton the white shirt. Her fingers had a blue tinge to them and shook so hard she couldn't work the small white buttons through their holes.

He swallowed. This was worse than the waistband. There were at least a dozen small white buttons marching down the front. Although it was loose fitting, there was the chance that he'd have to touch her chest to undo the buttons. He was chilled from the ride and the rain, but even so, Red began to sweat.

"Here, let me." Red's voice sounded gravelly to his ears. The memory of Laura telling him gravelly voices were alluring to women flashing through his mind didn't help his concentration toward his task.

He brushed her hands aside and tried to do the unbuttoning while holding the fabric away from her torso. The first couple cooperated. The next one didn't. He ended up pressing his fingers against her chest. Something hard met his fingertips. What was that? As the shirt gaped open, a quilted garment was revealed. There were metal hooks running down the front holding the sides together. Flat rods of some sort were what he'd been pressing against. This must be her stays. He'd heard of stays and corsets but hadn't ever seen one.

As soon as he'd finished, Red watched Gema take the

shirt off. Now, she stood with the quilted stays covering, well, from the swell above to the swell below and, thank the Lord, another white cotton gown underneath that reached to her knees. Red swallowed again and, taking off his Stetson, wiped the beads of sweat from his forehead.

Gema sat in the only other chair and began unlacing her boots. Though her hands were still shaking, as was her entire body, she was able to pull the strings from their holes. Red picked up the white shirt she'd worn under her bodice and tossed it over the wash line. He continued with the rest of the discarded items until the entire line was filled with dripping female garments.

When the second boot thudded to the floor, Red turned his attention back to her. Gema was rolling a black wool stocking down her leg. Red turned away quickly. Now, skin was being revealed.

He grabbed the Union suit from the pile of his clothes on the table and thrust it out, arm's length behind him, to her. "Here. You need to put these on. They'll be too big but will keep you warm."

They disappeared from his hand, and he breathed a sigh of relief. Fumbling and muttering, in what he figured was her native Russian, made him crack a smile. She was just as flummoxed with his garment as he was with hers.

Something he figured were her stays flopped over the back of the now empty chair. While more fumbling and mutters sounded behind him, he examined the stays.

The edges that had met in the middle were stiff from whatever the flat pieces were made from. Triangles of fabric were inserted along the top and bottom edges allowing more room for the swells of her body. The back was laced together with several inches of gap between the sides. There was a drawstring on what looked to be the top edge. Maybe she tightened it with that so it formed to her... Well, best not to think of those.

"Mr. Red?" Her voice was soft and tentative. He turned around. The Union suit swamped her. The neck gaped some but didn't reveal anything. A bit of white showed above the edge. He glanced at the chair. Nothing was on it but two masses of wet black wool and the stays. Must be her stockings. She must still have on the last, at least that he knew of, layer.

A glance at her feet showed no toes. The legs of the one-piece underwear ended far past her feet. The arms hid her hands also.

"Um, was that white, um, gown dry?"

"Chemise? Yes. Just very bottom damp. Okay." She shuddered.

Her hair was beginning to curl as it started to dry. Red grabbed a towel from a shelf and started wiping and blotting it. Gema took it from him and, in a moment, had it wrapped around her head with the hair all swaddled inside.

"Come." Red took her hand and led her to the bed. "Get in. I'll make coffee and heat up some stew. You try to get warm."

Gema nodded and climbed in as he held the covers up. He tucked them close around her. When he turned around, he looked up at the ceiling, then rubbed his hands down his face. *Why Lord? Why did you put me in this situation?*

~~~~~

Gema lay staring at the ceiling. She was so cold. Even in her native Russia, she didn't think she'd ever been this cold. There was no way she could stop her shivering.

Red had been so gallant, trying not to make her uncomfortable while she changed. She'd been so ashamed when she couldn't even get her bodice off. Then he'd teased her a couple of times, and the nervousness fell away. That's when she'd finally felt safe.

The day had been horrible. The worst in her life. Even worse than when her papa said he had to sell her violin. Her grandmother's violin. Babushka had begun teaching her when she was only six. By the time she was twelve, Gema was playing at festivals in the small village where they lived. The instrument had become hers, or so she thought, when her grandmother had died when Gema was fourteen.

That's when her father had decided to immigrate to America. The serfs had been emancipated in 1861, freeing them from the land. Rather than try to purchase the farm he worked, Gema's father decided to move his family to the other side of the world. That took money. Gema's violin was a major part of the financing. She felt it was a betrayal of her beloved Babushka. To Gema as well. The violin was a family heirloom, passed down through several generations, its tone becoming richer, fuller as it aged.

Her father had never realized his dream of homesteading in the rich prairie land of middle America. Just west of Dubuque, Gema's parents and siblings had contracted influenza and died, leaving the sixteen-year old alone in a covered wagon with the sum of her family's goods. She couldn't speak a word of English and understood few.

Gema was digging graves when a farmer came upon her. He'd buried her family and hitched his horse to the back of her wagon, taking her to his farm where his wife tried to comfort and find out what had occurred. The language barrier made it difficult for Gema to be understood, but finally she was able to draw on some brown paper what had happened. And get them to understand that she was only sixteen and alone. The following day, the farmer drove Gema to Sanctuary Place, Nugget Nate Ryder's mission for women in need, and left her there.

As terrified as Gema had been, reeling from the loss of her entire family, she was welcomed and supported by those who lived there. It had been a time of grieving, learning a new language and new culture, but at the same time of being loved by and loving the women and children she met. She still struggled with English and in times of stress lost the words she'd worked so hard to learn.

When the first group of Ladies journeyed to Stones Creek, Colorado the previous summer of 1868, Gema was offered the opportunity to be part of the group. Instead, she'd chosen to stay behind. One of the friends she had made during her tenure at Sanctuary Place was getting married in September. Gema decided to wait and go with the next group who moved. That opportunity had come more quickly than any had anticipated.

Libby Trembly came to the Place in November. She'd lost her husband and three young children in a steamboat explosion on the Mississippi just south of Dubuque. The young mother had been in shock when she'd arrived. Gema had developed a close bond with her. She knew what it was like to lose everyone you loved at one time.

The pastor and matron of the mission worried Libby might throw herself in the river, so deep was her grief. They called Gema into the office and explained their concern. They wanted to send Libby to Sanctuary House, hoping the move from where she'd suffered such a terrible loss would help her recover and start a new life. Would Gema go with her and watch over the grieving widow?

Gema and Libby had arrived in Stones Creek in January. It seemed the move had allowed Libby to begin to work through her grief. When the outlaw gang had attacked a homestead, killing the owner, leaving the widow, Lucy, and toddler twins behind, they were brought to Sanctuary House, and Libby had taken the grief stricken woman under her wing. Not long after, the measles epidemic struck. Lucy contracted the disease and died, giving her twins to Libby to raise.

Gema had contracted the measles too, but recovered. She'd gone back to her work as a maid in the hotel. Today, she'd been kidnapped by that outlaw gang the Ladies had been warned against as she left to go eat her noon meal.

She was in a predicament and knew it. First, would anyone believe she hadn't been accosted by the outlaws? If they did, it led to a second. Staying the night with Red alone in the line shack would certainly not be construed as innocent.

He'd been so careful not to see anything more than her outer layers of clothing. It had been funny really. The way he handed her the, what was it called? Union suit? And kept his back to her until she was dressed indicated she was most likely safe in his care.

What was going to come when she went back to Stones Creek? Gema wasn't going to think about that.

She shuddered. She wasn't any warmer. Her feet were freezing, as were her hands. Her backside felt as if it was sitting on ice. Gema knew she needed to dry her hair. That meant getting out of the bed and sitting by the stove. She wondered if Red had a brush. The tresses had to be a tangled mess. It would take a long time to work them out.

She closed her eyes, trying to stop her shivering.

"Miss Gema?"

Opening one eye, she saw Red holding a steaming mug. She sat up and reached for the mug. Maybe whatever was in it would help her get warm. Gema had to push the sleeves up to take the cup. The coffee was bitter, but it was hot, and warmth swirled down her throat and into her stomach. She took another swallow.

"Mr. Red." She'd had as much trouble with his name as he had with hers. They'd agreed soon after they met, while he was courting Laura, to use the title and first name when speaking with each other. "Must dry hair. Need brush, comb."

He pulled open a drawer in the stand beside the bed and took out a brush. When she started removing the blankets, he protested.

"You need to stay in here. To get warm."

"No get warm with wet hair. Need to sit by stove. Brush hair to help dry." Gema took the brush from him.

Red moved a chair closer to the stove. Gema unwrapped her hair as she walked over and sat down.

As she began working out the tangles, Red pulled the table in front of her. "I'm heating up the stew. We can eat while you brush. I'm not the best cook, but I can make a passable stew."

Gema smiled at him. The warmth from the stove was welcome but didn't seem to penetrate her skin. She was still shivering.

Neither spoke as he tended the stew, and she de-tangled her hair. Gema shuddered again. This time Red saw her.

"You're still cold?" he asked.

"Yes. Can't seem to get warm."

Red had folded the rest of the garments he'd taken off the line. Picking up a flannel shirt, he came to her. "Let me put this on you. You are used to many more layers than what you have now." There was a twinkle in his eyes.

Gema felt her cheeks flame. Too bad it didn't spread to the rest of her body and help her warm up. Red helped her into it, pulling it over her head. The sleeves were too long on this one also, so he rolled the cuffs back.

She flipped her hair out from the back as he moved to the stove. Red dished up two bowls of stew and brought them to the table.

"Are you any warmer?" he asked.

Gema couldn't suppress the shudder that shook her shoulders. That movement probably gave him the answer. She dropped her gaze to the stew.

They ate in silence. The awkwardness of the situation filled the room. Gema knew what the outcome of this night would be. Most likely, Red did too. Neither wanted to speak the words.

~~~~~

They'd finished the stew, and Gema was working on the tangles in her hair. Red could tell she was still very cold. Her hands trembled as she brushed. Every so often her entire body shook, her shivering trying to warm itself.

Red was standing behind her, leaning against the wall, his arms crossed over his chest. He'd placed the bowls in a bucket of water. They could be washed in the morning.

How was he going to suggest what he knew needed to be done? He'd been in a similar circumstance before when he and several other cowboys got caught out in a blizzard. It was awkward enough with men. But with a man and a woman— That just made their situation and its outcome even more inevitable.

He was still chilly but nowhere near how cold to the very core he knew she'd gotten. That was so very hard to relieve.

Red stood and rubbed his face with his hands. No point in putting it off. Gema needed to be warmed so she didn't succumb to lung fever. It was a real possibility. It looked as if her hair was dry. That was good. Having a wet head, everyone knew, could lead to lung fever. He moved in front of her and squatted down.

"Miss Gema? Are you any warmer now that you're all dry?" A violent shudder jerked through her. Red took the small hand that still had the bluish cast to it in his. "Miss Gema— Gema. There's a way to get you warm. I haven't suggested it before because— well, you're a woman, a single woman trapped here with me, a single man."

She lifted her eyelids, and the pool of her deep blue eyes studied his face warily.

"It's bundling. We share the warmth of the bed. Our body heat trapped beneath the blankets creates sort of a cocoon. My body heat will warm you."

Gema's eyes got wide. Shock was written on her face.

"No, honey. We'll both be fully clothed. You can even put on some of my trousers if you want." He pointed to the tan canvas pants folded on a corner of the table. "And socks. I have a pair you can wear. That will help you too." Red got up and retrieved the items.

Another shudder wracked her body as he set the garments in her lap. She needed to agree soon, or he was afraid she'd become ill.

"I—I need to— before." Gema's face turned bright red.

He figured out what her problem was. "Oh, yeah. I'll just go check the animals. There's the chamber pot." He pointed to the corner. Grabbing his coat and hat, Red donned them and fled out the door. He'd give her plenty of time to finish her business before he returned. He'd take care of his needs, too.

~~~~~

Gema stared at the door as it closed. What he suggested would seal their fate. Not that it wasn't already decided. That had happened when they arrived here at the line shack rather than going to the ranch homestead or to Stones Creek. Maybe she should have told him to take her home.

Gema didn't know how far the town was. It could be

too far away to get to town today. The vastness of the plains she and Libby had crossed coming to Colorado had reminded her of the Russian countryside.

No matter, they were here and wishing it was different wasn't going to change anything.

Gema took care of nature's call. It was a struggle to figure out how to use the drop seat. She put the socks on, then the trousers. The waist was too big and the hips a bit tight. She was slender, so surprised her. Red must be very slim hipped. Gema hadn't noticed that before. Not that she took note of men's hips. That wasn't proper.

Just as she finished braiding her hair, a knock sounded, and the door opened, admitting Red back into the cabin. When he took his coat off, turning to hang it and his hat on a hook, Gema couldn't keep her eyes from his backside. Her face flamed. Why couldn't her blushes lend their heat to her body rather than just her face?

She jerked her eyes up when he turned around. They stood staring at each other for a long moment. Red cleared his throat.

"Um, are you ready to bundle? I promise I won't do anything other than share my body heat." Red walked over to stand in front of her. "I promise."

"I promise, too."

Cracking a grin at her, he said, "I didn't think you would, but I'm glad to know I don't have to worry."

Red took her hand and led her to the bed. He helped her settle in and tucked the blankets tightly under her as she lay on her side facing the edge. He walked around to the other side and stood there. Gema waited. When he didn't get in, she looked over her shoulder at him.

"Mr. Red?"

His steel gray eyes met hers. He cleared his throat. "Um, I need to turn down the lamps." She watched as he did so, leaving one lit with the wick turned low. He used the boot jack to remove his boots and pulled his belt from the loops.

He came back around the bed and took a deep breath, letting it out slowly. Then, he lifted the blankets and climbed in.

The bed sagged, pushing them together. Red snuggled against her, his chest to her back. An arm slipped around her waist. Within moments, warmth began to seep through the layers of clothing between them. He tucked his feet around the ice that were hers. Very slowly, her shivering lessened.

Gema stared at the small flame in the lantern sitting on the table. She was so comfortable. Still cold, but not as much. This bundling was working. Her eyes drifted shut as she thought how protected she felt within the circle of his arms.

~~~~~

Holding Gema as they shared their body heat sent conflicting thoughts and feelings through Red. A woman's body pressed against his definitely felt wonderful, even with both of them fully clothed. He grinned in the darkness. She looked so funny standing there in his Union suit. In a way like a child dressed in a parent's clothing, hands, and feet hidden in the length of the sleeves and legs. But there was nothing childlike about the curves the red cloth outlined.

No siree.

Red liked that she was rather tall and slim, but with abundant curves in the places a man appreciated. In his mind, he pictured her expressive blue eyes. Set at a slant, they spoke of her Russian origins. Such dark blue, they looked like a mountain lake so deep you could never reach the bottom.

Red held her against his chest and felt her shivering lessen. The bundling was working. He said a prayer as he drifted to sleep, asking that she not sicken from her prolonged exposure to the wet and cold.

Sunlight easing over the windowsill brought Red to the awareness of a head tucked under his chin, an arm around his waist, and leg thrown across his hip. Seems that Gema had turned over during the night and decided he was pretty comfortable to sleep against. Red eased himself away and out of bed, being careful not to let too much cold air in. And the room was definitely cold.

Sticking his feet into his boots, Red moved to the window. His shoulders slumped. At least a foot of snow had turned the promise of spring back into winter. The only good thing was that since it was late March it wouldn't last long. Of course, when it melted, the ground would be a muddy mess.

It did make brewing coffee easy though. Red took the pot outside and scooped snow into it. He'd get a bucket to fill when he went to tend the animals.

Gema stood looking out the window when Red returned after his trip to the lean-to. The forlorn look on her face told him what he needed to know about her mood.

He could tell she was aware of their predicament. Knew what was to come when they were able to go back to Stones Creek. That wouldn't be today though.

The next day saw the snow melting. Red rode out for a short time to see if they could cross the creek that divided Hawk's Wing Ranch in two. It was high and rushing with meltwater. If it was just him, he'd go. But Red didn't want to take Gema across. Didn't want to risk her getting wet again. She didn't seem to be suffering ill effects of her drenching and prolonged cold.

"Tomorrow I'll go and see if the creek is down some. Maybe we can head to town then." They were eating beans and bacon for their supper. Gema had fixed them, complaining there was nothing to make them taste good. He'd laughed at her comment.

"We go tomorrow, no matter what. Need to get to town. My friends, they worry. Must show I'm okay." The look Gema gave him emphasized her words.

"We'll see. If it's too high, we won't attempt it. I won't risk us."

The next morning Red scouted the creek again and determined that they could head to town. There was more than just getting her back to her friends spurring him to the decision. Another night in bed with her had him dreaming of more than just bundling.

They rode to Hawk's Wing Ranch homestead to leave Milly, the donkey they'd brought along there. Hawk's surprise was evident.

"The deputy came by the other day asking if we'd seen anything. Glad you were able to escape, ma'am," Hawk said as a cowboy led Milly away. Hawk tipped his hat at Gema. "Juanita," Hawk yelled into the house. "She'll help you freshen up a bit before you head to town. Get a bite to eat, too, and some coffee."

A short Mexican woman came to the door. Hawk spoke in Spanish, and she bustled forward, grabbing Gema by the hand and pulling her to the porch, up the steps, and into the house.

"Red, she okay, really okay?" Hawk's concern was obvious.

"Yeah, a couple of women with the outlaws helped her escape. From what she told me, one decided she wasn't going to allow Gema to be raped and kept, so she got them drunk. Then, she and another woman took her away from the camp a ways and told her to run. She did. Even ran from me. Gema was in a total panic when I found her."

"You can give me the details when you get back. They're mighty worried in town. The blizzard kept the search parties in town. As soon as you get some grub in you, head to Stones Creek." Hawk eyed Red in a way that made him squirm. "You know what you gotta do, don't you?"

"Yeah. We haven't mentioned it, but I'm pretty sure she knows. I'll talk with the men while I'm in town. Don't think there'll be any problems. They let me court Laura. Even though that didn't work out, I doubt they'll object with Gema. Besides, there's no way for it not to happen." Even then, Red didn't say the word. Hawk didn't either.

CHAPTER THREE

CHLOE MCILROY heard the sound of hoof steps trotting up the street and glanced out the café window. The plates in her hand thudded to the tabletop. "Gema," she whispered, then she yelled, "Blanche. It's Gema, she's back."

Without stopping to take off her apron, Chloe ran out, letting the door slam against the wall as she threw it open. She ran along the boardwalk, past the storefronts of the businesses that shared the long building with the café and bakery. Mindless of the commotion her footsteps were causing, Chloe had one thought in mind. Get to Gema and see whether she was all right.

She'd been sick with worry for the past four days. First, when Gema went missing. Dread fought with worry when it was learned Mrs. Traci Fugard had seen a woman being carried across a saddle as the man riding whipped the horse into a faster gallop, leaving town. She hadn't sounded any alarm. Mrs. Fugard didn't approve of the Ladies of Sanctuary House. This woman was getting what she deserved for the loose life she'd led.

Chloe had slapped the bigoted woman across the face when she heard. Sheriff Newt Riverby had brought her to the House so the Ladies there could hear the words from her own lips. All the House Ladies in town, both the married ones and those who still lived there, were gathered seeking support from each other.

"You, no I won't say the word for what I think you are, Mrs. Fugard. You think you are better than we are because of your lily white past, and that many of ours aren't such. Well, let me tell you. Gema has a past just as clean as yours. She's simply an orphan whose family died, leaving a sixteen-year-old who couldn't speak a word of English. Sanctuary Place took her in. We loved her and helped her learn, not only a new language but a new alphabet, so she could learn to read. You didn't know Russians use a different set of letters and numbers, did you?

"We've all held her while she wept for her family?" Chloe waved a hand toward the other Ladies in the room. "We've helped her through the homesickness for anything remotely familiar to a young woman so far from all she knew. We've laughed with her when she messed up words. Helped her learn a totally new way to worship.

"Even if her past was like several of ours, no woman —" Chloe was shaking in her rage. "No woman, deserves to be kidnapped and raped. Don't gasp, Mrs. Fugard at my use of the word. It happens. No woman deserves that."

Chloe had burst into tears. Her husband McIlroy, who had come with the sheriff, gathered her in his arms and guided her out of the room.

Reaching the end of the boardwalk, Chloe nearly

tripped down the steps in her rush to get to Gema. The horse carrying her as she sat in front of a cowboy was stopping by the sheriff's office.

"Gema," Chloe yelled. "Gema." She ran as fast as she could up the muddy street. She needed to get to the young woman. Needed to know she was all right.

The man dismounted and lifted the young woman from his saddle. Who he was finally registered with Chloe. It was Red Dickerson. Gema ran to Chloe who embraced her.

"Are you all right? Did they?" Chloe couldn't say the words. She knew well what that gang of outlaws was capable of. The same thing had happened to her at a much younger age. She'd been held by them for thirteen years, being abandoned just before she went into labor. Nugget Nate and Penny Ryder, guided by one of his Callings, had rescued her and her eight-year-old son, Duncan.

"No, I escaped. A woman help me. Two women. Red find me. Got snowed in with blizzard. Just today good enough come to town."

"Praise the Lord. I was so worried." Tears streamed down Chloe's face.

Blanche Basking caught up then. She was the oldest of the Ladies at thirty-six and their leader. Blanche was also still without a suitor and so lived in the House.

She grabbed Gema from Chloe, hugging her. "Oh, Gema. I'm so glad you're here. We couldn't believe what happened to you. Snatched in pure daylight."

"Ma'ams," Red's voice broke into their reunion. "Sorry to interrupt, but I'm needing to get Gema in to speak with the sheriff. 'Sides, I don't want her to become a spectacle."

Chloe looked around. The boardwalks in front of the various buildings now had people standing and watching what was going on in the street. No one was moving except Noah Preston, the town's preacher. He was walking toward them, his long legs quickly eating up the distance. His black hat, black duster, and black mustache making him look like a gunslinger rather than a man of the cloth.

~~~~~

Red watched as Pastor Preston approached. As much as he admired and respected the man, Red just didn't want to talk with him just yet. He knew what would have to be done. Knew that Gema did too, though they hadn't spoken about it. The topic had been avoided during the time they'd spent snowed in at the line shack.

Sheriff Newt Riverby was watching the women. Noah had moved to stand next to him. Red caught their eyes and nodded. "Gema," Red said. He hated taking her away from the Ladies fluttering around her, but they needed to get the official reporting over with. "We need to talk with the sheriff." He didn't mention the preacher. They'd speak with him soon enough.

They settled in the office, with Gema seated in front of the desk, Sheriff Riverby behind, and the other men standing or leaning against the wall.

"Mighty pleased you're back Miss Volk…" The sheriff just let the rest of her name lapse.

"Please, just Miss Gema. Volkovichna too hard you to say."

"Fine. Miss Gema, I'm real sorry you had to go through such an ordeal. I'd like to ask you some questions if you don't mind."

Gema nodded. "Red, he say you will. It good to tell. I want those outlaws captured. Those poor women, poor children. So sick. Measles."

"What?" Noah broke into the conversation.

"Two women, one old girl, several young boy and girl. Several old boy. Many sick are the little ones."

The men looked at Red. "That's what she told me. I think Gema means teenagers when she says old girl and old boy."

Sheriff Riverby began questioning her again. Red helped where he could when she struggled to find the right words. The men's relief was palpable when they understood that she hadn't been assaulted.

When the questions were complete, Newt said, "Miss Gema, I'm sure you're eager to get to the House. The Ladies have been mighty worried about you. How about Red escorts you there?"

Gema jumped up from her chair and headed for the door. When she opened it, all the Ladies, both married and those still living in the House, were crowded on the boardwalk. Squeals, tears, and hugs sounded as the men watched.

"I don't think I need to be escorting Gema to the House, do you?"

CHAPTER FOUR

AS SOON as they were at the House, the Ladies hustled Gema into the kitchen. They set up the tub and began heating water on the stove.

"We figured you'd be wanting a bath. Such a terrible ordeal," Blanche said. She and Chloe had closed their café early.

As wonderful as it was to be back at the house, Gema didn't want to tell of her kidnapping and escape again. Especially about the three nights she'd spent in Red's arms. That Laura Duffle, Red's ex-betrothed, was listening made it awkward. Gema was no fool. She knew what was going to occur. The question wasn't if, it was when.

Gema told them about all that had happened. As she did, images of the events flashed through her mind. One in particular stood out to her. She leaped from her chair. "Oh, I remember. I must tell Red and Sheriff."

"What?" Chloe said.

"Sheriff ask if I remember any spots. What do you call them? Marks of land?"

"Landmarks," Laura said.

"Yes, landmarks. I remember waterfall. Tumbling down like it does." Gema pointed toward the creek that descended the mountain in a series of falls and gave the town its name. "I think it Stones Creek but then knew wasn't. I need to tell sheriff."

She ran out the back door, leaving the Ladies staring after her.

~~~~~

Red looked at Noah. He knew what was coming. He might as well let the man have his say.

"You spent three nights with Gema, alone in a line shack," Noah said.

Red nodded. He wasn't going to share the details of their bundling.

Silence stretched as the three men looked at each other. Finally, Noah spoke. "You're a God-fearing man, Red. Will you do what's right?"

Again, Red nodded. "I will. I didn't think I'd have any trouble convincing the committee."

As a safeguard for the women from his mission, Nugget Nate had set up a committee of four men who needed to approve any man who wanted to court one of the Ladies. He wanted them to make good lives for themselves and their children. Making sure the men they married were of good character was part of that. Besides the sheriff and pastor, Doc Eli Steele, and Ben Cutler, the owner of the general store, were those four men.

"No, you won't." Noah studied Red for a moment. "Seems God had a different plan for you than what you'd thought."

"You speaking of Laura?"

Noah nodded.

"I've learned a thing or two from her. I count her a good friend and hope she feels the same."

"You know she's betrothed to Hank now?" Newt asked.

Red thought about that news. He smiled. "I'm not surprised. I had a feeling he was interested. Didn't realize until after I'd committed to court Laura. I'm pleased."

Red watched some tension leave Noah's shoulders. The pastor's care and concern for his flock was heartening. "So, when are you wanting to have the ceremony?"

"Well, I'm not rightly sure." Red rubbed the stubble on his chin. "Gema and me, we haven't talked about it. She'd been through a pretty tough ordeal. By the time I found her, she was cold and wet. My concern was getting her dry and warm so she didn't sicken."

"Did she tell you about the measles epidemic?" Noah asked.

Red shook his head. "Just that some of the children in the outlaw camp had them."

Noah explained about the epidemic that had struck the town a month ago. Red had been at the line shack so hadn't heard the news. Many of the citizens of Stones Creek and the surrounding area had been stricken. When Noah told of Gema and Lucy Tanner, a young widow whose husband had been murdered by the outlaw gang, a tightness came into Red's chest. Hearing of Lucy's death clenched it even tighter. He sent up a prayer of thanks that Gema hadn't gotten sick from her exposure to the wet and cold.

The door to the jail office burst open. Gema ran in, panting in her hurry. "I remember. Landmark. A waterfall, like one here." She pointed.

Newt jumped up from his seat and looked at Red. "They must be near the line shack since you found Gema there. Do you know the falls she's talking about?"

Red stared off into space, scanning the terrain in his mind. "Yeah, I do. It's maybe a mile, mile and a half from where I found Gema."

"We'll get up a posse for tomorrow. Can you stay in town tonight so we can go first thing in the morning?" Newt took a rifle off the wall and began examining it.

"Sure, I've been away from the ranch homestead for a while, but I figure Hawk'll approve of this delay."

"I'm going too," Noah said. His tone brooked no argument.

Newt just nodded. "We'll take Dak. Do you think Massot would go? I'll ask him and Doc. We may need his skills if there are sick people."

"Yes," Noah said. "McIlroy will, too."

"You sure?" Newt asked.

"Positive." Though he didn't say anything else, Red got the idea there was more said in that single word than it implied.

"Okay, we'll meet here at dawn. Come armed and ready. Red, you escort Gema back to the House."

Red got the feeling Newt wanted him to speak with her about their upcoming nuptials but now was not the time. She was exhausted. He might not live through tomorrow. And right now, all he wanted was a bath.

~~~~~

Red stood just out of view of the front window of the barbershop. He wanted to gather his thoughts and feelings before he entered. The last time he was here had been when Laura gave him the mitten.

She'd really been marvelous in her anger. Red realized later just how far he'd stepped over the line in the comments he'd made that caused her to break their betrothal.

Red thought they were both a bit relieved that they weren't getting married. He knew he hadn't had the peacefulness that was settling within him at the thought of marrying Gema. Not that he was in love with the young woman. But something felt pretty right about it. At least he knew he was doing the right thing. The proper thing. Gema had gone through a terrible ordeal. She'd stayed with him three nights. They'd slept in the same bed. That would ruin her reputation.

Red remembered when Doc Eli Steele and his wife Leah had been kidnapped and trapped together by a bunch of jealous cowboys. Doc had done the right thing by her, and they seemed happy enough together. They had a baby boy now. Red couldn't remember the name, just that he'd been born shortly after Christmas. Laura had been excited about the birth. She'd told Hank first, understandable since he was in town and Red was on the ranch. It was a clue to Laura and Hank having a very strong relationship.

And that thought brought him back to the present. Hank and Red had parted friends after Laura gave him the mitten. Red had gone up to the line shack at the time, needing to be alone with his thoughts. Hawk had tasked him with looking for the outlaw gang while he was there. He'd just begun a more thorough search of the area when he found Gema.

"You gonna stand out here all day or come in. You look like you could use all my services." Hank had opened the door and stepped out on the boardwalk while Red was reflecting.

"How'd you know I was here? I stayed away from the window."

"You must have a lot on your mind." Hank pointed at the door.

Red chuckled. There was a window in the upper half. "Yeah, I do, on both counts. A lot on my mind, and I could use all your services."

They entered, and Hank told Red to take a seat in the barber chair while he checked on the heat of the bath water. Once he was done shaving and cutting Red's hair, he'd run the water from the boiler into the tub so Red could bathe.

Red cleared his throat as Hank came back into the front room of the shop. "I heard you and Laura got betrothed a while back. Congratulations. I'm happy for you."

"Thanks. We're planning on a May wedding. I'm working on some adjustments to my apartment." Hank pointed to the ceiling. "Massot gave me permission to expand over the café so the boys will have a room. Actually adding two rooms."

"How are the boys?" Red had been very close to the younger boy, Mark. Eddie, the elder, was closer to Hank.

Red had struggled to become friends with the lad. His jealousy of the boy's relationship with Hank was part of what led to his ham-brained words and Laura's reaction to them. She hadn't been very happy with Hank that day either. Seems they'd made up since they were betrothed.

"Well, I'm going to be beating you to the altar, after all."

Hank dropped the razor strop he held. "What? Who?"

"Miss Gema. I'm the one who found her four days ago. Just able to come from the line shack this morning."

Hank stood speechless. "You okay with that?"

"Have to be, but yeah. It's okay. Sort of has to be, don't it?"

Hank picked a wet towel out of the boiler on the stove with tongs and allowed it to drip into a bowl. "Well, my friend, I'll be praying for you and her. I wish you the best."

"Thanks, same to you and Laura."

CHAPTER FIVE

SEVEN MEN rode out of Stones Creek the next morning. Newt had deputized the five who weren't lawmen. His deputy, Dak Levine, passed out the badges. Noah gave a quick prayer that God blessed their cause to bring the outlaws to justice.

Since the hideout was on Hawk's Wing land, they went to the ranch first. Hawk Connor, the owner, and former US Marshal decided to go with them. He'd been hunting for them since he purchased the ranch the previous fall.

Red led them past the line shack, then up the hillside to the waterfall. They split into groups of two heading out to look for the cave Gema had described. Her description wasn't very clear as her view arriving had been from her position lying on the back of a horse, across a saddle. When she escaped, her focus was getting away as fast as possible.

The men gathered again after about an hour. Dak and Noah had seen some people. They weren't sure it was the gang. Newt decided that they'd all go to the location. If it was the outlaws, he wanted the strength of their numbers and their guns.

It didn't take long for them to come near to the spot. They dismounted and continued on foot, spreading out to approach from different angles.

As they drew near, it became clear these were not the outlaws. There were only four, and they were children who looked to be aged from about three to very young teenage. The oldest was in a hole shoveling dirt out with what looked like a tin miner's pan. A girl a little younger sat on the ground with a toddler on her lap. Another boy, younger than the girl, stood next to a bundle wrapped in a dirty cloth.

Newt silently signaled for the men to gather again at the horses. When they were all together he said, "I'm not sure what this means, but we need to scout around some more and see if there are others, adults, nearby. These kids could be bait to lure us out. Don't think so since the gang wouldn't know we were coming, but we need to be careful."

"I'd say the cave needs to be that way, uphill. There looked to be a spot off that way from where the children were," Hawk said.

Several of the other men nodded.

"Dak, Hawk, McIlroy, and I will do the scouting. The rest of you spread yourselves around the children, keep quiet and out of sight. We don't want to spook them. We don't know if they're armed."

As they moved out, Red wondered at the inclusion of McIlroy in with the other experienced lawmen. He knew the blacksmith had been in the War, but so had Red. So had Doc Eli. Red didn't know about Noah and Massot. It made no difference really, but the wondering passed the time it took to walk back to where the children were.

The oldest boy was out of the hole now. He picked up the bundle, jumped down into the hole. After setting it carefully down, he climbed out again. He and the other children began shoving the dirt back in the cavity.

"They're burying someone. Another child by the size," Noah whispered into Red's ear.

Red wanted to groan. Four children burying another wasn't something any child should have to do.

A who-hoot sounded. It was the signal to move in. The others must not have found anyone else. Red didn't want to go with his gun drawn but knew it was foolish not to. Any of the children might be armed. Maybe not the toddler, but all of the others could have experience with weapons.

Intent on their task, none of the children noticed as the men drew near. Then, the littlest one looked up and screamed. That made the others do the same. They began to scatter but were quickly caught. Though they struggled against their captors, strength faded and soon all the children were panting, subdued.

Noah approached McIlroy who was holding the oldest boy in his massive arms. "We won't hurt you, son. Will you tell me who you are and why you're out here in the wilderness?" he asked.

The boy tried to look tough, but then his lip quivered. "I'm Boone. That's Mae." He pointed to the oldest girl. "Tadpole, and the little one there is Nina. We just buried Boy." Boone pointed to each child, then at the half filled grave. He squirmed a bit in McIlroy's arms. Mae, Nina, and Tadpole all had fading rashes on their cheeks, evidence they were recovering from the measles.

"You going to run if I let you go?" asked the blacksmith.

"No, ain't no use. Yous bigger an' faster than me. 'Sides there's no wheres to run. Just back to the cave. Nothing there to keep up."

"What do you mean?" asked Noah.

"They done abandoned us once that new woman escaped. Took Ada with them, and Flora and Sally. Left us young'uns behind."

McIlroy swore. "Just like Chloe."

Boone's ears picked up the softly spoken words. "You know about Chloe? And Dunc? They's alive?"

McIlroy nodded. "Yeah, they were rescued way back when. Just as Lil-Pen was ready to be born. They live in Stones Creek. I'm Chloe's husband."

Tears and smiles fought for dominance on the boy's face. "They do?"

"Yes," Noah said.

"Will you take us to the cave? We'll gather what you have there and then head to Stones Creek," Newt said. When Boone began to look panicked, he continued, "You're not under arrest. We have a place there where you can stay, warm clothes, food, a bed."

"A bath," Dak muttered. The children did stink, but they didn't need to be told that. Each one was filthy and dressed in ragged, ill-fitting clothing. Long hair so oily and dirty that its color was hard to distinguish was tangled around the girls' faces. The boys weren't much better, though it was shorter. None had clothing adequate for the chilly, early April day.

"Noah, will you finish the burial? Hawk, Massot, go get the horses. We'll go with the children to the hideout and be back here shortly. Come on, you all. Let's go see to your things."

The cave was littered with a few blankets, a pot, bucket, and a small amount of food. A rag doll lay beside the fire pit. Nina squirmed to get out of Red's arms. He set her down. She ran and picked up the doll. Tucking it under her arm, she stuck her thumb in her mouth, then backed up to the cave wall.

"She's got what she wants," said Newt. "Anything else you young'uns want to take with you?"

Tadpole went to a blanket and flipped it back. There was a piece of wood that sort of resembled a horse. It wasn't carved. Nature had shaped it that way. It was worn smooth with much handling. Mae just looked around, not moving. Boone went to a pile of rubble. He dug around and pulled out a knife. It didn't have a sheath. He stuck it into the top of his ragged boot.

Eli was examining the food. "They only had about a day's provisions left." He looked at Boone and Mae, now standing close together. "Were they going to come back for you?"

Boone shrugged. Mae shook her head.

This time it was Newt who swore. "Let's go. If they do come, we want to be long gone."

At the gravesite, Noah stood praying over the filled in grave. The rest of the men were back with the horses. When they began discussing which child would ride with who, Mae backed away, turned, and began running.

Hawk ran after her and grabbed her around the waist, lifting her off her feet. "No need for that. We're just going on a ride to town."

"Mae's scared of horses. She got kicked bad once. Nearly died. There's a scar on her chest from the hoof." Boone had run to where Hawk was trying to calm the girl who was struggling in his arms.

Hawk wrapped his arms around her, pinning hers to her side. "Querida," Hawk said using the Spanish word for sweetheart. "I'll keep you safe on the horse. You'll ride in my lap with my arms protecting you the entire way. I promise I'll keep you safe. Will that help?"

Mae looked at him, then at Boone who gave an encouraging nod. She looked back at Hawk and nodded. She wrapped an arm around his neck and allowed him to carry her to his horse. "You stand here by Boone while I mount. Massot, come lift her up."

When Mae was straddling the saddle, Hawk took hold of the reins on either side of her. Mae took hold of one hand and pulled it around her body.

"You want me to hold you tighter?"

Mae nodded.

"Okay, querida. I'll hold you as tightly as I can."

Hawk looked down at Boone still standing close by.

"She don't talk anymore. Not since…" Boone let the sentence drop.

Hawk bit back a curse and nodded. "Head off and get a ride. We need to get a move on."

~~~~~

64

Newt listened as Boone talked. The boy sat in front of him as they rode to town. Without Newt asking more than an introductory question, Boone had begun telling about his life with the outlaw gang.

He'd been born in the gang. His mother, Prue, had died two weeks earlier in the measles epidemic. Boone's voice broke when he told of that. Several others had died, too.

"They took Ada when they left. Flora tried to get them to leave her behind, but they wouldn't. Said that since the new woman escaped, Ada could just be shared more between them. They'd beat up Flora for being meddlesome. I thought they was gonna kill her when they woke from their drunk and found the woman gone.

"Is she okay? That woman?"

"Yes, Miss Gema was found and is back in Stones Creek," Newt said.

"Good." Boone was silent for a long while. "Will I, we really have beds? And enough food? And clothes enough to keep us warm?"

"Yes, we'll see that you do."

"Do ya think I'd be able to learn letters and to cipher? My Ma could do both. She'd read the papers the men brought back. She tried to teach me an' Ada to read, but we never had a book or nothin' to write on. I know some of the letters. Ma taught me numbers, too. I can count all the way to twenty."

Newt's heart broke at the simple desire for warm clothing, food, and a bed. Basic needs of all people. And Boone wanted to learn to read. How many children complained about having to go to school? Newt had as a child.

"Dunc's really in Stones Creek?"

"Uh huh. You know him?"

"Yeah, we played some before they left him and Chloe at that shack in the woods. I just figured they died. She was gonna have another baby. Did it die like the others?"

"Lil'Pen's alive and a real happy little girl. Chloe's married to him, McIlroy." Newt pointed to the man who had Tadpole in front of him. "He's teaching Dunc to be a blacksmith." Newt chuckled. "You ask him about the time he shot McIlroy."

Boone jerked around and looked at Newt. "Dunc shot him?"

"Uh huh. It's his tale to tell so I won't spoil it for you."

"I'd a been killed for sure if I shot one of the men."

"You know how to shoot a gun?" Newt asked.

"Been known to some. Phil was teaching me. He said I'd need to know for when I started going on jobs."

"That what you want to do?" Newt asked.

"Nah. I can't see that robbing is a good way to live. You're always looking out for the lawmen. You never have enough to eat. You're always too cold or too hot or too wet. You can't ever stay in one place. Always trying to stay one step ahead of the law."

"What do you think you want to be?"

"I reckon being a cowboy would be good. Somebody cooks your meals. You got a bed in a bunkhouse. A horse that's your own. Plus you most likely don't get shot at much, unless there's a outlaw gang around."

Newt thought that was probably true. It seemed to him

that the boy had a good head on his shoulders. There might be hope for him, if they could find someone to take him on to raise. He'd like for it to be a married couple. Hawk might be a good choice, but he wasn't married.

Red would be a positive influence as well, but with his upcoming marriage to Gema, Red would be trying to build a life with her. They didn't need the challenge of a young teenager. Besides, Red didn't have any experience with children. Neither did Gema that he knew of.

Newt ran the rest of the ranchers in the area who might possibly take on the boy through his mind. He rejected each one. There was something in each situation that didn't seem to allow for adding a possibly very troubled teenager into the mixture. Well, he'd just have to pray about it. God would supply Boone just the right man to guide him into adulthood.

~~~~~

The children's arrival at Sanctuary House caused a massive upheaval. Between moving two more beds into the room two of Blanche Basking's boys occupied, one in with Katherine Naylor, Ruth's twelve-year-old daughter, and one with the twins Libby Trembly was now raising, several men were allowed onto the upper floors long enough to complete the task.

Blanche supervised the furniture adjustments. Libby dug through drawers and trunks to find unused clothing that would fit the four strays who had landed on their doorstep.

Ruth Naylor fried up sausage, made gravy from the

drippings, and baked fluffy biscuits to fill empty bellies.

Eli and Red took Boone and Tadpole to get clean in Hank Johnson's bathing tub. Hank would give them haircuts, too.

Nina bathed in a washtub normally used for laundry, set on the kitchen table aided by Libby. Mae would take her bath in the washroom with Katherine helping wash her hair.

Mae looked at the dress she was supposed to put on and began to cry.

"She never had such a purdy dress before," Nina whispered to Libby who was helping her out of her ragged clothing. "Me neither."

The dress was plain and worn as several girls had outgrown it. Still, it was better than the one Mae had on. The one for Nina was the same.

Both girls were small for their ages and thin. Their bones stuck out all over their bodies. Their hair hung in lank, greasy, tangled strands.

Katherine came into the kitchen from the washroom shortly after she and Mae began her bath. The four women who lived in the house were in the room, all busy with various tasks. "Mama," she said to Ruth. "Mae's scrubbing her skin so hard I'm afraid she'll start bleeding."

Ruth dropped the utensils she was putting away. Everyone looked at her. She'd gone pale. "Let me tend her, Katherine. You take over my chores. First, go get Chloe. I know she's at the café, but she'll want to see Mae. She'll be able to help, too." Ruth looked at the other Ladies in the room. They knew why Ruth was so affected by her daughter's words. Knew why she wanted Chloe, too.

"I'll go," Blanche said. "I can finish closing up."

Ruth went into the washroom, closing the door behind her. The girl sat in the tub with a bar of soap clutched in one hand and a washrag in the other. She was scrubbing the inside of her thigh with brutal strokes. "Mae, let me help you wash. You'll rub your skin raw, and it won't help. I know." Ruth went to take the cloth, but Mae jerked it out of reach, shaking her head violently.

Mae turned and looked at Ruth, eyes ravaged with soul-searing pain met hers. Tears clogged Ruth's throat. At least she'd been older when she'd been raped. This little girl was way too young. Chloe would understand better than anyone. She'd been about the same age when she was kidnapped by the same gang.

The back door opened, and Chloe stepped in. Mae took one look at her and burst into tears. She dropped the soap and rag and held out her arms to the first familiar face she'd seen since the gang had abandoned the children.

Chloe dropped to her knees and embraced a child she hadn't seen in over five years. "Mae, Mae, how did you come to be here?" Mae buried her face in Chloe's bosom, weeping. Chloe looked at Ruth.

"The posse—" Ruth had to clear her throat before she could continue. "They went out this morning and found four children abandoned by the outlaws. Mae is one of them. She was scrubbing herself raw. I know how she feels. I figure you do, too."

"Oh, honey." Chloe held the girl to her, stroking her hair. She kissed the top of Mae's head. "It'll be okay. We understand. You let us help you wash. Then we'll get you dressed." Chloe leaned back and took Mae's face in her hands. "You're safe here. No one, and I mean no one, will ever be allowed to do that to you again."

Gently, with words of comfort and support, Ruth and Chloe cleansed the frail, thin girl. Mae's sobs lessened under their tender care. Both women knew what Mae had endured. Chloe especially. Time, love, and a safe place to heal was what she needed. That was the mission of Sanctuary House.

CHAPTER SIX

RED KNOCKED on the front door to Sanctuary House. Boone and Tadpole were standing beside him. He didn't think they'd ever been so clean before. Both boys had loved the warm water and wanted to soak longer. Tadpole squirmed in the barber chair, but Hank was patient and finally managed to get his hair cut. Boone just stared at everything. Neither boy had been to town very often. Most things were new to them.

Ozzie Basking, Blanche's thirteen-year-old son, answered. "Wow, you clean up real good. You even have blonde hair. I couldn't tell before," Ozzie said to Boone. "Come on in."

Red allowed the boys to enter before him. He stepped into the foyer and looked into the parlor on the left of the staircase and the large dining room on the right.

Libby came with Nina in her arms. The little girl was clean also and in a new-to-her dress.

"Afternoon, Mr. Dickerson. I see you brought the boys back all spit-shined." She smiled at each one.

"I did at that, Mrs. Trembly. Nina looks all clean and

shiny. Sleepy, too."

"I'm just heading upstairs to put her down for a nap." She eyed Red. "Is there something I can do for you?"

Red took off his hat and circled the brim in his hands. "Um, would you please ask Miss Gema if she would be so kind as to speak with me in the parlor?"

Libby tipped her head to the side. "I will see if she's awake. We've encouraged her to rest as much as possible. The ordeal took a lot out of her, and she was barely recovered from the measles."

"Thank you, ma'am. I'm most appreciative." Red went into the parlor to wait. He paced the length of the room several times before Gema appeared in the doorway.

Red stepped to her. "Gema, um, Miss Gema." Red glanced behind her to see if any of the children or Ladies were within hearing range. None were. "Will you please come and sit so we can have a conversation?" He bent slightly at the waist and extended his hand toward the settee.

Gema sat on the edge, her back straight. Red sat beside her. He rubbed his hands on his pant legs. Turning to face her, he took one of her hands in his.

"Gema, we haven't discussed anything about what happens now that we're back in Stones Creek. Please know that if I could have brought you back here that first day, I would have. You know how impossible that was. Until today we couldn't get past the creek. That means we were there three nights together."

Red watched as a blush rose up her neck, blooming across her cheeks. "I—I— Gema, will you do me the honor of becoming my wife? I pledge to be a faithful husband, and if God blesses us, a loving father." There, he'd gotten the words he'd practiced over and over in his head out.

Red thought he saw glistening in her eyes, but Gema quickly blinked it away.

She nodded. "Yes, Red, I will marry you. Be a faithful wife and if God blesses, loving mother."

~~~~~

Gema tried to relax her back, but it stayed stiff as if a rod was buried inside. Red had proposed, as she knew he would. They had to marry. They both knew it. It was the only solution to their having spent so much time alone together. And they'd slept in the same bed.

That hadn't been so bad. Red was like a warming pan that lasted the entire night. Each time she'd roused in the night, she'd been plastered against him with an arm or leg or both hugging him tightly.

"When will we do ceremony?" she asked.

"I suppose it depends on how much of a party you want to have with it? The fancier, the longer it will take to prepare."

"No," gasped Gema. "No party. Just marry. No need pretend we in love."

Red nodded. "No party. Won't take long then. I'll need to talk with Pastor Preston." He rubbed his face. "I need to get back to the ranch. Hawk's waiting at the jail for me. Today's Saturday. I'm not sure I'll be able to get back to town for services tomorrow. I've been away from the ranch a long time. I'm thinking next Saturday might be best. We can stay the night over at the hotel. After worship service

Sunday, we can head back to Hawk's Wing."

Gema nodded. She watched a flush color Red's cheeks.

"That'll give me a chance to get the house cleaned up and ready for you. I'm not much of a housekeeper."

Gema grinned. "I know. Line shack pretty messy."

~~~~~

Gema had never expected to marry for love. That rarely happened in her culture. She had thought the man who proposed to her would actually want to marry her, however. That wasn't the case with Red. They were marrying because they'd been alone together. A rather silly reason, if you asked her. It showed very little faith in the character of the couple. Seemed to pander to the gossips. But, the attitude was the same here as in Russia.

Red was gone. He'd left shortly after they'd agreed to marry the following Saturday. Since he and Hawk had to get back to the ranch, Red was going to speak with Pastor Preston and set a time for the ceremony. The pastor would come and let Gema know.

Gema had adjusted to the less formal style of worship here in America, so she figured she could adjust to their form of wedding ceremony, too. She'd only been to one wedding in America before. The Ladies could answer any questions she had.

Gema bit her lip. She had to tell the Ladies she was getting married in a week. Should she wait until supper, or tell them now? All those who lived at the House were there now. She knew the twins and Nina were napping. Ozzie and the other boys were showing Boone and Tadpole around. Mae had been put to bed, also. She had looked extremely tired when Chloe and Ruth escorted her to her new room. She didn't know where Kathryn and Nancy were, but it really didn't matter. They all had to be told anyway.

Gema went to the kitchen. The two girls were there, as well as Laura, Blanche, and Chloe. "Nancy, will you tell mother and Libby come, please."

Everyone looked at Gema.

"Kathryn, you and Nancy stay upstairs, so if Mae or Nina need something, they won't be alone and scared," Blanche instructed.

The girls scampered off. All eyes turned to Gema. The atmosphere in the room had been thick when she came in. Now it bordered on oppressive. Was the advent of the children's arrival creating a burden? Gema didn't think so. At Nugget Nate's mission, any who sought sanctuary was welcomed.

Ruth and Libby arrived, their expressions questioning. They stepped to where the other Ladies sat around the table.

"I make announcement," Gema began. "Mr. Red request we marry. I say yes. We marry next Saturday. Then I leave for Hawk's Wing Ranch. No party."

Blanche stood and came to hug Gema. "I'd say congratulations, but I'm not sure you want to hear that. Blessings on your future, Gema."

Each of the Ladies expressed their felicitations. Laura approached last. She hugged Gema close. "He's a good man, Gema. He'll treat you right."

Confused, Gema said, "But you end betrothal? I

thought you not like Red."

Laura gave a small chuckle. "Oh, I was hopping mad at him that day." She paused. "I think God had a hand in that breakup. If I hadn't given him the mitten, Red wouldn't have been at the line shack. Then no one would have found and rescued you. Maybe those outlaws would have gotten you again.

"God's mercy might have been at work in saving Red and me from a marriage He knew wasn't the best for us. And saving you by having Red at the right place and time for you." She grinned. "Red just might have learned something about women through our courting and break up. Now, if he gives you any trouble, you just come and find me. Between Hank and me, we'll make sure he knows what's what."

~~~~~

Pastor Preston, Doc Eli Steele, and his wife Leah came to Sanctuary House after supper that evening. Noah came to tell Gema when the wedding ceremony would be held on the following Saturday. Doc wanted to check on the four children now living at the House. Leah came to speak with Gema.

Since Doc was using the parlor to examine the children, Leah and Gema went up to her room. Not knowing why the woman would seek her out made Gema nervous. She offered Leah the only chair in the room, but she chose to sit on the bed beside her.

"I'm sure you don't understand why I want to talk with you. Know that I only have your best interest at heart." Leah took Gema's hand. "You're scared and worried and unsure right now. You feel as if your life is out of control, taken over by some force that is pushing you into a whirlpool where you'll drown."

Gema's eyes widened. How could this poised woman know exactly how she felt?

"I was in the same place you are. Eli and I had to marry because of a situation much like yours." Leah went on to tell of their kidnapping and imprisonment in a cave a few miles from Stones Creek. They had been trapped there for three days and nights before Nugget Nate Ryder found them, enabling the town men to unblock the entrance. Penny Ryder had spoken to Leah in much the same way she was to Gema now.

"So, you see, if you go into this planning to be a good wife, respecting Red, being faithful and true to your vows, I believe you can grow to love each other. Penny said she and Nate did, and it's obvious to everyone their devotion to each other. Eli and I have, too.

"Oh, we have our squabbles. Every couple does. Sometimes I want to throttle him. He is a man after all, so that comes with the territory. He probably wants to do the same to me.

"What it all boils down to is this, if you go into the marriage determined to make it work, God will bless you. Red is a good, God-fearing man. That he and Laura are still friends is evidence of that. Scripture says a cord of three strands is unbreakable. Between you, Red, and God that's one strong cord."

Tears slipped over and down Gema's cheeks. She wasn't alone. Someone else understood how she was feeling. How scared and uncertain she was. That she would fail to be a good wife and that Red would come to resent her. Leah taking the time to come and speak with her gave Gema reassurance that maybe, with God's help, she and Red would come to love one another. Would have a long and happy marriage.

"Will you pray with me?" Gema asked.

"Of course."

They knelt beside the bed. Leah prayed in English for the young woman and Red. Gema started in English, then, with an apology to Leah, switched to her native Russian. The words came so much easier then as she poured out her fears to the only one who could truly ease them.

~~~~~

Lying in her bed later that night, staring into the darkness, Gema thought about her future life with Red. She would do all she could to be a wife and maybe someday a mother. It was the duty of a woman, after all, to provide her husband with heirs. Living with the variety of women who came to live at Sanctuary Place, Gema was aware of what went on between a man and woman and how those children were made. The thought made her terrified and excited at the same time.

She knew he was a man of good character. How he treated her so very carefully while they were in the line shack spoke of that. That he was messy was evident, too. The thought made her grin. He'd learn a thing or two from her on that score. Not that she'd nag, but her mother always said, "Start the way you intend to continue." If Gema didn't want to live in a messy house her whole life, Red had better… What was the expression? Toe the line.

CHAPTER SEVEN

THE LADIES wouldn't let Gema have her way in having no sort of celebration to honor her marriage. On Tuesday, they cornered her after supper and told her what was going to happen on Saturday, and they were brooking no argument.

Rather than have the ceremony at the church, it would be held at the House. The dining room would be rearranged by the husbands of the married Ladies. They'd pushed the time for the ceremony back to late afternoon.

After the wedding, they would have supper and cake. All the Ladies would be in attendance. Even Birdie, who had married a rancher with three children, was going to be there.

When Gema saw how much it meant to the others to make the day festive, she agreed to their plans. She worried that Red would show up expecting an early afternoon wedding and be upset the time had changed.

Ozzie Basking offered to ride out to Hawk's Wing Ranch and let them know. He'd been learning to ride a horse as he worked after school at the livery. He'd gotten into trouble recently for riding to the ranch and not returning until the next day. Blanche had been frantic since Ozzie had neglected to ask his mother's permission.

With the strict admonition to return as soon as he delivered the message, Ozzie was going to ride to Hawk's Wing the next day after school. The dire consequences he'd face if he failed to do as instructed wiped the grin off Ozzie's face when his mother agreed.

Once the children were put to bed, the Ladies gathered in a storeroom on the third floor. In it was the crate shipped with Gema and Libby when they arrived in January. Those still living at Sanctuary Place had embroidered linen sets to be given when one of the Ladies married. It was Gema's turn to choose.

Ruth and Libby helped take the sets from the crate. The ones Gema wanted were near the bottom. "These." She held up a set. They were not well stitched. Flowers were askew. Stitches were irregular and crooked.

"Why would you want those?" Ruth asked. "There are much nicer ones." She held up a pillowcase.

"Betty made these. When I came to Place, Betty so kind. She hold me while I cry. She help me learn to speak. She like Mother two. I miss her. She put love in stitches, even if not pretty."

"Then these are perfect for you. Special memories. You'll think of Betty every time you use them."

"I go write to her and tell her about Red, and that I take her linens."

Blanche gave Gema a hug. "You're a sweet young woman, Gema. Red is lucky to be getting you as a wife."

~~~~~

Gema looked at her face in the small mirror on the wall of her room. This was the last time she would get dressed here. In a few minutes, she was going to walk down the stairs and marry Reddington Dickerson.

She learned his real first name just yesterday when Laura asked if she knew it. It surprised her that he had a different name than what she knew him by. These Americans were a strange people. They sometimes even called a man by letters rather than a name. The banker was called C.J. His real name was Chalmers Jehosaphat Ritter. And they all thought her name was hard to pronounce!

It wouldn't be her name much longer. She would be Gema Dickerson.

They had all been so very supportive this past week. Pooling the few coins each one had, Myra Riverby, who worked at Mrs. Steele's dress shop, purchased braid and replaced the ribbon decoration on Gema's good gown. When the Ladies gave it to her, she broke into tears. She was so surprised, as they hadn't told her they were doing it.

She loved them all. Only Libby hadn't been a resident at the Place when she'd come to live there. Each woman held a spot in her heart. They'd all helped a sixteen-year-old who couldn't communicate deal with grief and fear, showering her with love and acceptance. It was one of the reasons she moved to Stones Creek when offered the opportunity, even though it meant traveling across the plains in the winter. The other reason was helping Libby begin to heal from her terrible loss.

A knock sounded at the door. It opened, and Ruth stuck

her head in. "They are ready for you to come down. You look lovely."

Gema felt panic rise, threatening to close her throat. Ruth must have noticed because she entered and hugged her.

"Wedding jitters. Everyone gets them. Or so they tell me. Never having been married, I don't really know. You'll have to tell me about them when it's my turn."

The comment made Gema laugh, and suddenly her fear was gone. She was still nervous but didn't feel like she was going to faint anymore. Picking up her Bible, she exited the room that would no longer be hers.

~~~~~

Red stood at the foot of the stairs watching Gema descend. When she reached the bottom, he would offer his arm, and they would move into the dining room, between the Ladies, their children, and the husbands of those who were married.

Gema was beautiful. Far too beautiful for the likes of him. Blonde hair piled up in a more elaborate way than he'd seen before, even on Sundays. Those fathomless, dark blue eyes set at such an exotic angle. She was above average in height and with a shape any man would admire.

But she was so young, only twenty. Red was thirty-four. How could such a young woman be attracted to someone who was almost old enough to be her father? Not that Red's thoughts were at all fatherly.

Gema stepped down to the floor, her eyes locked on his. They had been the entire way. She was nervous. They'd only known each other as more than passing acquaintances for less than two weeks. Now, she was his bride. No wonder she was looking at him like a scared rabbit.

As much as he wanted to, Red decided they wouldn't fulfill their vows tonight. He would wait until she was comfortable with him. Maybe in the meantime, he could encourage an attraction between them. Or her attraction to him since he was definitely attracted to her. Now that it was allowed, of course.

Red extended his arm. Gema placed her hand on it, and they walked into the dining room and to where Pastor Noah Preston stood waiting.

~~~~~

Red locked the door of the hotel room. When he turned around, Gema was standing beside the bed, wringing her hands. She was so nervous she was trembling. It reminded him of when they were at the shack and trying to get her warm. This time she wasn't cold though. She was terrified.

Walking up to her, Red took her hand. He noted that her glove was worn and mended. He'd have to be sure to have her purchase new ones, or maybe he could give some to her as a gift. But he didn't know what size.

He knew she didn't have many belongings. He and Hawk had loaded her trunk on the wagon he'd brought to town. It was small and light. Red had always heard women had lots of clothes. Gema didn't, it seemed. Maybe that was a way he could encourage her to like him, buy her new clothes.

Hawk had driven the wagon back to the ranch since it

looked as if it were going to rain. Red would rent a horse from the livery tomorrow for Gema to ride when they left town. Hawk had left his horse, Hania, for Red to use.

"Gema, honey, don't fret yourself. It'll be okay. We won't do anything tonight. Or maybe not much of anything. I know you're nervous." He didn't want to use the word afraid. She might not be, and he didn't want to suggest that she should be. "I would like to kiss you though. That peck at the ceremony wasn't how a man should kiss his wife."

Gema visibly relaxed. "I'm sorry so nervous. Just so much changes so fast."

Red drew her gloves off one finger at a time. Her hand trembled a bit, but he didn't know if it was from fear or a more pleasurable feeling. He knew it was affecting him.

"I'm going to leave for a few minutes so you can change." He encircled her with his arms and kissed her with gentle desire. The last thing he wanted was to scare her with passion. "Then we'll bundle like we did at the shack. The only difference will be fewer layers of clothing."

~~~~~

Gema quickly changed into her nightgown. She used the chamber pot and slipped into bed. Now that Red had promised not to... well... just not, she relaxed. At least she knew which side of the bed he slept on and that he didn't snore. That was far more than most brides knew on their wedding night.

Was she being fair to Red in not consummating their marriage? Maybe not, but there was no way she'd be able to relax if she thought they were going to...

A knock sounded, and the door opened admitting Red. "Did you know there was a bathing room just down the hall?" He sat down on the other side of the bed and began removing his boots.

"Yes, I work here as maid. Clean many times. Men filthy pigs."

The firmness with which she said the words caused him to chuckle. "Who told you that?"

"I see, but other maid tell me words. They very true."

"I suppose so." Red took off his cutaway sack coat, laying it across a chair. He began unbuttoning his vest.

"I not see that coat before. It new? You not wear to Sunday service."

Setting the vest aside, he eyed her and swallowed. "Um, yeah. It's new. I, um, ordered it a while back. It came in last week. Just picked it up from Ben's store. Haven't had a chance to wear it." He knew he was spewing words but couldn't seem to stop them.

"You order for wedding of you and Laura." Gema's tone was matter of fact, easing his concern.

"Yes."

"Nice coat. Nice vest. You look well."

"Good."

That confused her. He could tell by the look on her face.

"You look good, not well."

"I good. Feel fine."

Red started laughing. He dropped on his stomach across the bed and gave her a quick kiss. "The way you tell someone you like how they look is, 'You look good,' or 'handsome.' You look well means someone doesn't appear ill."

"Ah. You look good and well." Gema suddenly blushed.

Red realized he was lying partly on top of her. He got up quickly and turned away to unbutton his shirt. Now that he knew she was watching him, Red was embarrassed to be undressing in front of her. Gema probably didn't realize he'd never done so before.

There was only one lamp lit, and it was on Gema's side of the bed. The wick was high, so there was plenty of light. Should he ask her to turn it down or out? Or would she think he was empty in his upper story? No help for it. He'd have to either ask or walk all the way around the bed to do it himself.

"Gema, will you please turn down the lamp?" Red didn't face her to ask as he unbuttoned the final button. The room dimmed as she did so. He slipped his suspenders off his shoulders and unbuttoned his trousers, then slipped them down his legs, folding them and placing them on the chair with his coat and top-shirt.

Leaning over, he untied the tapes on the legs of his drawers and took off his socks. He removed his shirt and undershirt and dug in his bag for his nightshirt. Letting out a soft breath, he pulled it on over his head. When it settled around his knees, Red slipped off his drawers. Nothing left now but to get into bed.

At the shack, they'd slept in the same bed out of limitation and need. Now, it seemed odd to join her there. At least it was dark. Maybe it was the fact that they each only had one layer of clothing on: Gema in her nightgown, him in his nightshirt.

Red slid in between the sheets and lay on his back beside her. "Goodnight, Gema."

"Goodnight, Red." Gema turned onto her side facing away from him.

He stared at the ceiling.

"Red?"

"Yes?"

"I'm cold."

Red smiled, turned, and snuggled up to her back, wrapping an arm around her.

~~~~~

Gema and Red ate lunch at the House the next day after worship service. They were heading to the ranch that afternoon. Red had described the house he lived in as foreman. It was small, just three rooms, but it could be added on to when they had children. That statement had caused Gema to blush a deep red.

"Gema, honey, while you change from your Sunday-go-to-meetin' dress, I'm going to get Hania at the livery and rent a horse for you." The startled look on Gema's face stopped his words. He took her hand and drew her close. "What's the matter? You know we're heading out to the ranch today, don't you?"

"Yes, yes. Not that. It…it… I not ride. Not know how. Please, no." She gripped his hand so tightly her knuckles turned white, and her nails dug into his skin.

"It's okay, honey." He wrapped an arm around her shoulders. "Would you rather ride double with me?"

The relief on her face gave him the answer. "Please,

yes."

"You go get changed now. I'll be back faster than a jackrabbit can spit." Red gave her shoulders a quick squeeze, then strode out the door.

As he saddled Hania, Red smiled. Gema didn't seem to mind his touch. They'd woken up this morning pretty much the way they had each morning at the shack: a tangle of legs and arms.

This time he hadn't had to carefully extract himself so she wouldn't be embarrassed by their position when she woke. Instead, Red lay with soft curves pressed against him, his arms holding her to him. That is until she woke up, jerked in surprise at how they were arranged, knocking her head against his chin, clicking his teeth together. Thankfully, he hadn't bitten his tongue. She'd laid very still for a long time, relaxing in his arms.

Now, she wanted to ride double with him. It wasn't that unusual for a woman to ride behind a man on a horse. They'd hold onto his waist either astride or sidesaddle. Red hadn't ever thought that looked very safe or all that comfortable for the woman. Besides, having Gema in his arms while they rode was appealing.

He planned to teach her to ride, but for now, he'd rather she rode with him. If she could ride and she went off alone, there was always the chance of the outlaw gang finding her. Gema staying close to the ranch homestead minimized the chances of her being taken again.

The smile left his face as he tightened the cinch. That gang needed to be captured. Not only had they kidnapped Gema, but they'd abandoned four children to die in that cave. Red and Hawk had met with Wes Chase and Linc Pierce of the Chasing R Ranch the previous week. They'd discussed methods of searching their ranches and the surrounding lands for signs of the gang as they and their men went about their normal activities. Red prayed the gang would be found quickly.

Gema was waiting outside on the porch when Red rode up to the House. The Ladies, as well as most of the children, were there as well. As he dismounted, general hugging and words of farewell were exchanged. Ozzie Basking held Hania's reins while Red tied Gema's valise onto the back of the saddle opposite his.

"Come on, honey." Red took Gema's hand and said goodbye and thank you to the Ladies. "You'll ride in front like we did coming from the shack." The smile she gave him said she approved of the position.

Red gave her a leg up, and when Gema was settled, he mounted. The fit with both of them in the saddle was snug. This time he didn't have to worry about propriety. He could pull her close to him. Then again, that might not be such a good idea.

Ozzie handed him the reins, and with a wave, Red kicked the horse into motion.

~~~~~

Gema sat stiffly in the saddle. Red had an arm around her waist and was holding her close against him. When they'd ridden from the shack, both had tried to keep whatever little distance they could between them. She knew Red had sat on the back slope of the saddle then. Now, however, he was more down on the seat.

"Gema, relax, or your back is going to ache by the time we get there."

Red's words startled her out of her thoughts. How could she say she was nervous about them being so close together? She thought of how they had been when she woke up that morning. Her cheeks flamed. At least he wouldn't be able to see since her bonnet shielded her face from view.

Gema thought back to their mornings in the line shack. She knew they had slept tangled together there, too. She just hoped Red didn't know. Each morning she had awakened before it was light, needing the chamber pot. When she got back in bed, Gema had laid on the edge of the bed, as far from Red as she could get. Since he was always gone when she next awoke, Gema was certain he never knew they cuddled so close in the night.

"Come on, Gema, lean back against me. It's fine. We're married. It'll be more comfortable for both of us."

Even though he couldn't see her face, Gema shyly dropped her head a bit and relaxed. She leaned back and rested against his chest. His arm tightened around her waist.

"That's my girl."

Gema thought she felt a kiss on the back of her head, but through the bonnet and her hairdo, she wasn't sure.

CHAPTER EIGHT

IT HAD only been a week, but Gema loved living on the ranch, at least so far. They had been welcomed by Hawk Connor, Red's boss, Alberto and Juanita Valdez, the head wrangler and housekeeper, as well as all the cowboys. Red had been teased about how pretty Gema was, and why she'd marry someone like him who was as ugly as a mud fence. She hadn't understood since she thought Red was quite handsome, though she'd never tell him.

Hawk invited them to have supper with him and the Valdez's that evening. He told Gema that if they wanted to eat with them every meal that would be acceptable. He'd appreciate it if she helped Juanita whenever they were going to be joining them.

During the week, she and the Mexican housekeeper became acquainted. Juanita didn't speak English and had a difficult time understanding Gema's. They'd begun to use some hand signals to communicate.

Inspiration struck, and Gema began saying the names of everything they used. Soon, Juanita was learning the English words and Gema the Spanish. They laughed a lot at their mistakes. Now, Gema knew the Spanish word for every vegetable they planted in the garden and Juanita knew the English.

It was late afternoon on Sunday. Red had gone to tend to some chores. Gema was wandering around the homestead, getting ready to shoo the chickens into the chicken house for the night. Music floated from behind the bunkhouse. Gema abandoned the chickens and ran to the end of the building peeking around the corner. Red had asked her not to invade the cowboy's areas. They were a rough lot, and might not watch their language as well as they should around her.

Oh, how she wanted to approach the man who she thought was named Jeb. He was playing a violin. It was poorly tuned, but he was playing with enthusiasm. She thought the song was something about camptowns and races. It was one she was familiar with from Sanctuary Place. The words she'd never been able to follow, but the tune was lively, and everyone danced to it.

"Well, missy, you like the fiddle?"

Gema startled and looked at the man standing behind her. It was Cookie. His name said it all. He was the cook for the cowboys. Big in height and girth, gray-haired, with a shaggy beard, he'd helped with planting the garden. Rather than a wide-brimmed cowboy hat, Cookie wore a bowler.

"Yes, I play. Played before we come to America."

"Well, come on an' grab the fiddle and bow from Jeb and show us how it's played in Russia." Cookie reached for her hand, but Gema tucked it behind her.

"Red, not want me with cowboys. Say they too rough

speak."

Cookie chuckled. "He's surely right about that. They wouldn't know how to palaver with a lady. Let's go find Red and get his okay for you to spend a bit of time with that fiddle." He grabbed her by her other hand and steered her toward the stables.

"Hey, Red," Cookie hollered when they entered the dimness.

"What?" Red came out of a stall, closing the gate behind him. When he saw Gema standing in the doorway, he hurried forward. "Is something wrong?"

"Naw, your little lady here heard Jeb squeakin' on that there fiddle of his. Seems she knows a thing or two about playing. Thought she might be a wantin' to give us a song or two on the thing. Wants you to give her the okay to be around the cowboys."

Gema bit her lip as Red approached, wiping his hands on a rag. "Is that right? You know how to play a fiddle?"

She nodded. "I play grandmother's, then when mine. Papa sell to help pay for coming to America." She desperately wanted to have a violin in her hands again but would abide with whatever Red said.

"And you want to try playing again?"

She nodded, clenching her teeth against the disappointment when he said no.

"Well, come on. Let's go see if Jeb will give the thing up for a few minutes so you can play something."

~~~~~

Red didn't know what hit him. All he'd said was that he'd take Gema to Jeb and see if she could play his fiddle.

Now, he had her in his arms, and she was crying on his shoulder as she held him tightly. He looked at Cookie who smiled at him.

When she quieted, Red escorted her to where the cowboys were gathered. "Jeb." Red waited until all the cowboys were looking at him with Gema who was standing slightly behind him, gripping his hand tightly. "Seems my wife can play the fiddle. Would you be of a mind to let her use yours to show us?"

Jeb who was sitting on a log stool jumped to his feet. "Sure enough, Red. Be glad to. My arm's gettin' a might tired." He held the violin out, and Red took it.

"Here you go, honey. Give it a whirl."

Gema took the instrument and bow. He watched as she stroked the wood, her face held an expression of love and joy. Tucking it under her chin, Gema touched the bow to the strings. Several minutes were spent tuning them to her satisfaction. Then she stepped back, centering herself within the semi-circle of seated and standing cowboys.

At first, Gema ran through several sets of scales, pausing to start over when her fingers stumbled. Then, she began a haunting, sad tune that brought echoes of the past to Red's thoughts. He glanced at the other cowboys. They were feeling the effects of the music, too.

Once the strains of the song faded, Gema picked up the tempo with a lively folk song that had the men all smiling. Red could tell she missed some notes, but that she had a natural talent was obvious.

She played two more songs he wasn't familiar with. Then, she played another piece evoking emotions of joy and sorrow, love and loss. Her eyes were closed, and tears streamed down her face. He couldn't take his eyes off her. Gema seemed one with the violin and bow. They were extensions of her body. When Gema lifted the bow from the strings and bowed her head, Red looked at the cowboys. They were opened-mouthed at the wonder of the music they'd just heard.

Gema stepped up to Jeb. "Thank you for opportunity to play." She held out the violin and bow so he could take them back. She turned away and walked to Red. "Thank you. Can't know how much a gift you gave me." She hadn't bothered to wipe the tears away.

Red watched as she walked away, heading toward their house.

"She's mighty talented with that thing. Much more than Jeb," Cookie said from his spot leaning against the bunkhouse. Several of the cowboys voiced their agreement. Others were teasing Jeb about how much better Gema played than he did. He was nodding.

Red glanced at the men. "Thanks, Jeb. It seems to have meant a lot to her."

"Any time she wants to play, you tell her she can, even if I'm out on the range and she wants to practice. I'll show Cookie where I keep it. He can get it for her."

"Much obliged to you, Jeb." Red tipped his hat and walked away, following in his wife's footsteps.

He found her lying on their bed, weeping into her pillow. "Gema, honey, are you okay?" He sat beside her and stroked her back.

She turned her head. "Yes, fine. So lovely to play again.

It been so long. Miss it so. Memories, good memories. My grandmother, my babushka. She teach me. From very little girl, I play. Then she die. Papa want move to America. Sell my violin. No can play then."

"You truly love to play, don't you?" Red asked.

Gema rolled onto her side. "Yes, the music, it in here." She touched her chest. "It wants come out but no can. Hum, not enough. Sing, not enough. Not know words America songs. Russia songs no others know."

Red realized then that Gema hummed often. While she cleaned, cooked, did laundry, any of the activities of daily life. She hadn't at the shack, but she'd been under a great deal of stress.

He'd stayed close this past week, not riding out on the range. He wanted to be sure she settled in well. She and Juanita were becoming friends, even with their limited communication skills. Cookie was keeping a careful, fatherly, eye on her, also.

Tomorrow, Red was going to have to head out with the cowboys. He'd been gone longer than he'd anticipated when he went to the line shack.

"Jeb said you can play his fiddle whenever you want. Just ask Cookie if he's not around."

Tears glistened in Gema's eyes. She wiped them away and chuckled. "I water pot today. No more tear. I plan special thank you for cowboys for let me play violin." She kissed him. "Special thank to you for let me." She kissed him again.

"Honey, any time you want to thank me like that you go right ahead."

Gema's face turned bright red.

Over the next two weeks, Red spent most of his time away from the homestead with the cowboys as they rode the range. There were many nights he spent out under the stars wishing he was home in bed with Gema. Not that they had progressed in their relationship in a physical way. They still slept curled around each other but never went further than snuggling.

As attracted to Gema as Red was, he didn't want to push her. He was so much older than she was, and that held him back.

~~~~~

Gema stood on the front stoop of their house and watched as Red went to stand beside Hawk. They were watching Jeb accustom a young horse to a saddle. At least he was here at the homestead. He'd been gone so much, riding the range. She understood the need to round up the calves for branding, but sometimes he was staying out for two or three days at a time. How could they get closer and eventually make the marriage more than one in name only if he was always gone?

Gema was more than attracted to Red. She'd lie beside him at night and hope he'd turn to her wanting to do more than cuddle. Their bodies seemed compatible. They woke up each morning a tangle of arms and legs.

Gema had taken Jeb up on his offer of playing his violin. She'd taken the sheet music from her trunk that had traveled with her all the way from Russia. The precious papers, wrapped in oilcloth, were given to Gema shortly before her grandmother's death. Yellowed with age, they held fond memories of holding the instrument and bow during many hours of practice. Scales, solo pieces, duets. Folk music and classical. Many were hand copied, the ink fading, the paper brittle.

She played during the day, practicing after her chores were done. In the evening, she and Jeb would trade off playing for the cowboys. Red seemed to be proud of her. He complimented her as they walked back to their house. Gema hoped each night he would turn to her, that he would do more than kiss her lightly on the cheek and say good night.

Maybe she needed to be a bit bolder. Gema had kept away from the corrals, barns, and stables, not wanting to be in the way. Maybe Red didn't think she was interested in his work. Maybe if she spent small amounts of time with him when he was here, he'd see that she wanted to be a larger part of his life.

With that goal in mind, Gema stepped off the stoop and approached the two men leaning against the rail fence.

~~~~~

"Hawk, I'd like to discuss something with you," Red tipped his hat back a bit. Hawk looked at him, so he continued. "I heard tell that Mrs. Trembly is looking to sell the Tanner place to help with the twins."

"Heard that too. Such a tragedy. Silas murdered, then his wife dies of the measles. Mrs. Trembly's taking them on is a blessing. Mrs. Basking said having the twins to take care of was helping the woman with her own grief."

They watched the horse jump and buck, trying to get the saddle off his back. Jeb had a talent for gentling horses.

Red and Hawk had confidence the horse would be saddle broke by the end of the day.

"So, you interested in the Tanner spread?" Hawk asked.

"I'd like to own it. I can't begin ranching it on my own though. I was hoping you and I could strike a deal." Red sent up a silent prayer that Hawk would agree to his plan. "I can buy the place with a good down payment. I've been saving for a long time. I don't have enough to build a house and outbuildings or buy much stock. I'm hoping to raise horses first, then move on to cattle."

"You want to stay on as foreman?"

"Yes, I'd like to stay on and also buy a few of your young mares. I'd brand them as mine but keep them with your herd. We could run them all on my place for grazing. I'd also like to use your studs until I can buy one of my own. I'd pay you stud fees when the time comes."

"That's a sound plan," Hawk said. They went on discussing the details of the arrangement. Red would go to town the next day and speak with the new lawyer in town to set up a contract between Red and Hawk concerning the particulars. He'd also meet with the banker, who was also the land agent, about buying the ranch. When the topic was exhausted, they watched as Jeb worked with the horse.

~~~~~

Gema approached the two men quietly from behind. She didn't want to interrupt them if they were discussing something important.

"You and Gema getting along?" Hawk asked.

"Yeah."

"Married life agreeing with you?"

Red was silent.

"That bad, huh?"

"No, it's not bad. Not exactly. It's just... There's something holding me back from getting closer to her."

"Oh?"

"I'm not sure Gema wants me, if you know what I mean. She's so very young. Nearly young enough to be my daughter. How can she want an old geezer like me?"

Gema stood stock still. Red thought she didn't want him? Nothing was farther from the truth. The truth was, she did want him. Yearned for him, but didn't know how to let him know.

Slowly, so as not to let him or Hawk know she'd been there, Gema backed away until she was far enough, then turned and hurried back to the house.

Inside, she paced from the stove in the kitchen and through to the fireplace in the parlor. There was also a small washroom at the back entrance and their bedroom. Not a large area to pace in, but she managed.

"Red doesn't think I want him," Gema mumbled in Russian. "That I think he's too old. Stupid man. He's not old, at least not to me. I think he's very handsome.

"He also thinks I'm very young. Well, I'll show him I'm a grown woman. A woman who wants to be a wife. His wife. I'll..." Gema stopped pacing. She had no clue what she'd do. She knew what the ultimate goal was, but not how to get there. And there wasn't anyone on the ranch she could ask. Juanita was the only other woman. Though they were making progress with English and Spanish, neither woman was proficient enough to help Gema with her dilemma.

For that, she'd have to go to town. There was one of the Ladies who Gema knew would be able to tell her how to make her husband see her as a woman, a desirable woman: Myra Riverby.

The problem was: how could she get to town? She didn't ride. Had no clue how to drive a buggy or wagon. It was too far to walk.

The clock on the mantle bonged the hour. They were eating supper at the main house tonight. It was time for Gema to go help Juanita begin supper. Maybe, between now and when they were gathered around the table, she'd think of how to get to town in the very near future.

CHAPTER NINE

GEMA SAT in front of Red on Ralph. She didn't think she'd ever want to learn to ride or drive. She loved being in the saddle with his arms around her. It made her feel secure, maybe even desirable, with Red's arm around her waist and her back against his chest.

Gema couldn't believe her good fortune when Red announced, at supper, he was going to town the next day. She'd immediately asked if she could ride along. She made up excuses about things she needed to purchase. When Red said he knew she wanted to see and talk with her friends, Gema barely kept her mouth from dropping open. Did he know what she was going to talk with Myra about? No, he couldn't. He must just be thinking she missed the other Ladies. While that was true, it wasn't the reason she wanted to go to town.

"Gema, I didn't get a chance to tell you about why I'm going to town today. The hogs getting out of their pen messed up our evening. Believe me, it's no fun trying to round up escaped pigs in the dark."

Gema chuckled. Red hadn't come home until after

she'd gone to bed.

"I'm planning on buying the Tanner place. I have plenty of savings for a good down-payment. I'm staying on as foreman on Hawk's Wing. Hawk's going to sell me five mares, and we'll run them with his herd. We've got it all arranged. It'll be several years before I can build a house and barns, but it's a start to my own ranch. I'm talking with the banker and the lawyer today. You should have plenty of time to visit with whomever you want. Put whatever you want to buy on my charge."

Gema nodded. She wasn't planning on purchasing anything unless Myra thought of something she needed to accomplish her purpose. She smiled to herself. Red didn't know it yet, but their marriage was going to an entirely new level tonight.

~~~~~

"I'll leave you here and go do my business with the banker and the lawyer. I don't know how long it will take. How about I meet you at Sanctuary House?" Red asked. They were standing in front of Cutler's General Store. Ralph had been stabled at the livery.

"Yes. Will be there. Going to talk with Myra first. She at dress shop maybe. I go see."

"See you later, then." Red descended to the street, heading to the bank.

Gema entered the dress shop owned by Leah Steele, wife of the town doctor, Eli. The bell above the door jingled.

"One moment," said a voice from the back room. It wasn't Myra's. Gema didn't know if she was relieved or disappointed. She wanted to get the discussion over with as soon as possible, but the topic wasn't one to be overheard while it was going on.

Leah Steele came into the room carrying her son, Steven, born in late December. The boy flashed a wide grin at her.

"Good morning, Mrs. Dickerson. How may I help you?"

"Good morning. Is Myra here? Want to see her." Gema waved her fingers at Steven, who grabbed at them.

"Watch out. He bites. He has two teeth now." Leah smiled at him. "She's not here today. Troy wasn't feeling well, so she stayed home. I'm sure she'd love to see you."

"Thank you." Gema said goodbye and left the shop, heading to Sheriff Riverby's house. Myra hugged Gema when she answered the knock.

"Come in. I'm so glad to see you. We all miss you so much. You being out on the ranch and all." Myra led the way into the parlor. Troy was upstairs napping. Myra made tea, and they chatted about Hank and Laura's wedding that had occurred the previous Saturday.

"So, how's you likin' bein' married?"

Gema swallowed. This was so embarrassing. To actually speak to someone about the lack of the physical aspects of being married was much harder to do than think. "Much is good. Juanita, very good friend. I teach English her. She teach Spanish me."

Myra began laughing and had trouble stopping. "You're teachin' English. That's just 'bout as bad as me a tryin' to. Twixed my back hills Tennessee accent an' my messed up grammar, ain't no way I'd be tryin' to teach somebody to talk right."

Gema realized how strange it was for her to try and help someone learn the language. It was working though. Juanita had added many words to her English vocabulary. Many more than Gema had acquired of Spanish. "Yes, strange, but work much good."

She waited until Myra's giggling subsided before bringing up the topic she wanted to discuss. "Have problem. You help, yes?"

The smile on Myra's face vanished. "Is he hurting you? You just say the word, and we'll get you away from him."

"Oh, no, no. Red good man. He good husband. He want good for me." Gema took a deep breath and said, "He not think I want him. He... I... We not... He think he too old. Me too young. Stupid man."

"Well, that dog won't hunt. You want to..." Myra circled her hand, not saying the words.

"Yes, not know how show Red I want. You help?"

A sly grin grew on Myra's face. "Yeah, I can help. We's gonna be real subtle 'bout it. You been working a lot in the garden, right?"

Gema drew her eyebrows together, puzzled. "Yes. Much work planting seeds. Hoeing."

"So, your arms is real tired and sore. It's real hard to reach behind and untie your corset strings."

"But tie string bow in front." Gema didn't understand.

Myra let out a frustrated breath. "I know, but you want him to get close enough and to touch you, right? So you need to give him a reason. Tying the bow in the back gives you a reason."

"But, seems like lie. I no hurt."

"Well, chop some wood." Myra waved her hands in the air. "You'll hurt. You got a greater purpose here."

Gema fought between disappointment and delight. She was beginning to understand what Myra was getting at. That she probably wouldn't accomplish her goal tonight was a delay she didn't want but could handle. Then again, if they got back to the ranch early enough, Gema could do some hoeing and chop some kindling.

"I get Red untie strings, loosen laces. He get idea?"

"Maybe, depends on how stubborn he is. Don't move away when you take your corset off. Then…" Myra went on describing some ways to encourage Red toward the ultimate goal.

When Gema left, she headed to Cutler's General Store. She was going to purchase a sweet smelling lotion for Red to rub onto her sore arms and back.

~~~~~

Red was in a good mood. Arrangements to purchase the Tanner spread were begun with C.J. Ritter, the banker. Forsyth Franklin Fredrick Farnsworth the Fourth, the new lawyer in town, was going to write up a contract between Red and Hawk, outlining both sides of their agreement. Red would soon be on the way to owning his own ranch.

Gema sat in the saddle in front of him, tucked close to his chest. Once they'd left town, she'd pulled his arm around her waist and still held his hand as they rode back to Hawk's Wing.

She was chattering about her visits with the Ladies she'd

seen. They'd had lunch at the café, enabling her to chat with Blanche Basking and Chloe McIlroy. Gema had even made a small purchase: lonament, as she called it. He thought she meant liniment. When he'd inquired about it, she'd blushed and mumbled that her arms sometimes got sore from working in the garden and other chores.

Red had made a purchase, also. An order, actually. He was keeping it a secret, but knew Gema would like it. Like the Stetson hat he'd bought last year, it was expensive but would last her a lifetime.

Ben Cutler had told Red the news about the completion of the Transcontinental Railroad a couple of days earlier. A gold spike had been the final one driven, connecting the Union Pacific and Central Pacific Railroads.

Another stop Red made was to the jail. He'd asked Sheriff Riverby if there was any news about the outlaw gang who had kidnapped Gema and abandoned the four children. There wasn't, but he said the children seemed to be adjusting to living at the House fairly well.

Mae, who still wasn't speaking, was becoming attached to Blanche Basking. Boone was very protective of her. Nina cried for her mama quite often, who the Ladies had found out from Boone was the woman named Sally.

Tadpole, Mae's brother, was curious about everything in the House and town. He would turn up at various shops or homes, coming in without knocking which upset most of the women. Newt had sat him down, explaining some of the rules of society and how Tadpole had to obey them. After that, the boy mainly stood outside the homes and waited until he was invited in, or loitered on the street looking in the shop windows.

Ruth Naylor began teaching the older three their letters and numbers. None wanted to go to school since they had no background in learning and were having to start out at the very beginning. That helped keep Tadpole at the House rather than on the prowl around town.

Red rode up to their house, letting Gema dismount. She glanced up at him. "Thank you, for taking me to town. Was good to see the Ladies."

"Anytime, honey. If I can get away from the ranch, I'll take you to town whenever you want. I'm heading to the main house to talk with Hawk about what I got done today. I'll see you at supper."

For some reason, which Red couldn't figure out, Gema blushed and lowered her eyelids.

~~~~~

Gema went into the house, knowing she'd acted strangely. She could see it on Red's face. Later on, he might like what she was keeping from him. She unwrapped the bottle of lilac-scented lotion. If Myra was right, this might be what tipped the scales toward Gema and Red becoming husband and wife in every sense of the words.

Changing into her work dress, Gema went out with her hoe and worked her way down five long rows in the garden. The seedlings were small, so she had to be careful not to hoe them up. Then, she moved to the wood pile. They needed kindling, didn't they? It was needed for all the stoves and fires on the homestead. Gema chopped small logs into splinters until her muscles ached. Now, she could honestly tell Red she hurt and ask him to rub the lotion onto her back and arms.

Juanita came out of the house, took one look at the sweating young woman, the ax in her hand, the pile of kindling, and shook her head. "Come, chica, bath."

Gema soon found herself in the bathing room of the main house in a tub filled with warm water. Juanita scolded her in a mix of mostly Spanish with a few English words sprinkled in. Gema caught the meaning and had to hide a grin. Red wouldn't like his wife working so hard it made her sore. Wouldn't be happy she was too stiff for loving.

Although it wasn't a day they normally ate at the main house, Juanita sent word to the stables that Red should come there for supper. She wouldn't let Gema do very much to help prepare the meal.

Gema was seated at the table in the kitchen when Red, Hawk, and Alberto came in. Juanita met them at the door to the mudroom and chattered in Spanish. Gema knew the housekeeper was complaining about her doing so much hard work. Chopping wood was a man's job. If Gema thought they needed more kindling, Red, or one of the cowboys should do it.

Red came and squatted down in front of Gema as the others moved into the dining room. "Honey, you didn't have to chop wood. I know this is a busy time of year for the cowboys, but if the kindling was low, I would have set one of them to chop it."

Gema was touched by his concern. She laid a hand on his cheek. "It not matter. Done now. Plenty for many days." She stood up, and a groan she hadn't known was coming escaped. She was sore. Very sore. More sore than she'd planned on. Maybe she had chopped too much wood. She might need Red to rub that lotion into her muscles for real. Gema just hoped she was not too sore to accomplish her goal.

~~~~~

Juanita had shooed Gema away when she began stacking dishes to take to the kitchen. "Go home. Rest. You sore mañana." Another spate of Spanish followed. She turned to Red and began giving him orders. At least that's what it sounded like to Gema.

Red folded his napkin and laid it on the table. "Come on, honey. I've been told to take you home and make you rest." He placed a hand on the small of her back and escorted her out the door.

Gema was glad to be heading home. She hurt all over, especially her arms. They ached. If she had to raise them over her head, she didn't think she would be able to.

Red used the boot jack once they were in the house to remove his boots. Gema watched with envy. Her boots were laced. His simply slid off when the heel was pressed against the boot jack. She was going to have to bend down and unlace them. Her muscles protested at the thought. Sighing, she headed to the bedroom. Red followed.

While Gema was unbuttoning her work gown, Red changed into his nightshirt. It was almost beyond her to ease the garment off her shoulders. It fell in a heap around her feet. There was no way she was going to bend over and pick it up. It could lie there until morning.

"Honey, can I help you? You look pretty stove up to me."

"Stove up?"

Red chuckled. "Sore, stiff." He began unbuttoning her corset cover. "Seems like we've been in this position before." Red grinned at her. Gema grinned back.

"Not cold and wet now," she said.

"No. There," he said, slipping the last button through its hole. "Let me unlace your boots." He knelt and soon her shoes were set under the edge of the bed with her stockings rolled up inside.

"You haven't made much progress on that corset cover while I slaved to get your boots off," Red teased.

"Too stoved up."

"Let me help."

Red helped remove her corset cover and petticoats. When they were set aside, Gema turned her back to him. "Please help with lacings. I not reach."

While he worked the strings, Gema began to giggle. Soon she was laughing.

"What's so funny?" Red pulled the laces loose, and Gema undid the hooks holding the front sides of her corset together. She tossed it onto the dresser and wrapped her arms around him.

"My plan. It not go as I want. My fault. All my fault."

"What plan?" Red held her close.

"Plan to show I want you as wife want husband and husband want wife. Talk to Myra. She help with plan. Plan you help with corset and rub lonament on sore arms and back. Showed some ways to make you, as she say, on fire. Not want to lie. Work hard to make some sore. Work too hard. Now stoved up."

Red pulled back and studied her face. "You want…"

Gema nodded. "Very much want old geezer." She giggled.

"You heard Hawk and me talking?"

"Yes. Come to spend time to show interest. Hear you. Make my plan." She sobered. "Now plan spoiled."

Red drew her close, tucking her head against his chest. "Your plan isn't spoiled, honey, just delayed. Believe me, as soon as you aren't stoved up, we'll make sure your plan works out."

~~~~~

Red helped Gema off Ralph's back after he'd been tied to the hitching rail at the church on Sunday. Worship service would begin in a few minutes. She linked her arm with his.

Gema saw Myra Riverby entering the yard holding her son's hand with Newt following close behind. Myra turned and gave Gema a questioning glance. Gema just smiled and winked.

CHAPTER TEN

SHERIFF NEWT Riverby was studying the new wanted posters that had arrived that morning. The jail door opened, and three women he didn't know walked in. Two looked to be in their late twenties. The third couldn't be very far into her teens. Their clothing was ragged. They were dirty and thin. He stood.

"Ladies. How may I help you?"

"We come needin' help, Sheriff." The woman who spoke was large framed but thin, with brown hair and eyes. "We done walked from the King Gang camp. We escaped. We's wantin' asylum. I think that's the word. Protection from the men." The woman who spoke had a large bruise on her cheek. The other woman had red marks on her neck. The teen stood behind the other two as if she were trying to hide.

Newt was dumbfounded. These women had just walked away from the most notorious outlaw gang in a two-hundred-mile radius. Then he realized that, if they'd walked away, the gang couldn't be very far from Stones Creek.

"How'd you get here? I know you walked, but how did you find the town?"

"We could hear the trains in the distance. Figured the tracks must not be that far. The men left to go rob somethin'. Don't know what. They never say. We waited a while, then headed out. Found the tracks an' followed them. That were yesterday. Figured they'd come to a town sometime."

Thoughts flew through Newt's head. They must be hungry. Tired. The gang had to be close. Close enough for the women to have walked here in one day. They needed a place to stay where they'd be safe. He needed to gather up a posse to hunt the gang. They might already have fled the area if they'd gone back to their camp and found the women gone.

Newt realized he'd never asked their names. "Ladies, will you tell me who you are?"

"I'm Flora Potter," the brown-haired woman said. "This be Sally Rife." She pointed to the blonde. "An' she's Ada."

Newt waited for a last name. When it didn't come, he remembered that the children didn't have last names. They'd all been born in the gang. Ada must have been, too.

"Sheriff?" This woman, Sally, was smaller, a little on the short side. Her hair, which like the others was pulled back and tied at the nape with a thong, might be blonde. It was so dirty and oily it was hard to tell. The teen's hair looked to be red under the grime.

"Yes?"

"Did that Gema girl get back?" Sally twisted her fingers

together. "When it done started to rain an' snow we got worried about her."

Newt grinned a little. "Yes, a cowboy found her and brought her back. She's well."

The women hugged. Their joy at the news evident. "It were all worth it then. All we took was worth it." It was Flora who spoke.

"What'd you take?" Newt was afraid he knew but had to ask.

"Nothin' we weren't used to. Just harder and more often." Flora's gaze dropped to the floor.

He looked at the marks on the women and gritted his teeth.

"That were part of why we left. Other part was the kids. T'weren't right to leave 'em in that cave all by themselves. Leavin' 'em to die."

The blonde began to cry. The teen hugged her.

"Ladies, we found some of them. Four. They were burying one."

Sally broke Ada's hold and grabbed Newt's arm. "Who'd you find?"

"Mae, Tadpole, Boone, and Nina. They are all well."

Sally collapsed onto her knees, sobbing. "My Nina, my Nina. She's alive."

Flora knelt beside Sally, patting her back.

"What about Boy?" Ada asked. Newt could tell she already knew the answer. There were tears in her eyes.

"The children were burying him when we found them."

Ada stared at the wall. The tears now slid down her face. "He were my little brother. Ma died of the sickness.

Sophie Dawson

Boy took it real bad. He got sick and didn't seem ta want ta go on. I hated ta leave him, but the men wouldn't let me stay." Ada wiped the tears from her face with a dirty hand.

It suddenly occurred to Newt that these women would want to see the children. Sanctuary House would be the best place for them to stay, also. He pulled his pocket watch out and checked the time. The café would be closed now. Blanche should be at the House. Chloe might still be cleaning the café, but she could be fetched quickly.

"Ladies, let's go to where the children are. I'm sure they'll be delighted to see you. We'll make arrangements for your housing, too."

Sally rose and wiped her nose with her sleeve. Ada put her arm around her as they left the jail.

~~~~~

Newt led the small procession across and up the street. He made a quick stop at Preston's Gun Shop, alerting Pastor Noah Preston about the advent of the women, and asking him to get Chloe Ashburn from the café. The women huddled against the side of the building. Newt noticed several townsfolk standing around staring at them.

"Head on about your business, folks. Nothing to concern you," Newt called. He escorted the women to the next street over to Sanctuary House, knocking on the door. The women tried to tuck themselves behind him.

Blanche Basking opened the door. "Afternoon, Sheriff. What can I do for you?"

Newt tipped his hat. "Ma'am. I've got three women here who're needing what this house gives— sanctuary. They escaped the King Gang yesterday and walked to town. Not sure how far it was, but I'm sure they need food and shelter. Will…"

Blanche cut him off. "Of course, come in." She brushed Newt aside and gently pulled the women into the house. "Come to the kitchen. We'll…"

This time it was Blanche who was cut off as they entered the dining room. Mae and Tadpole rushed past her, hugging Flora and Sally. Boone flew past, embracing Ada.

The back door slammed, and Chloe ran into the room. "Flora. Sally. Oh my word, Ada. Praise the Lord." She hugged one, then another, then the last, repeating the hugs several times. Tears flowed down the cheeks of everyone, including Blanche, Ruth, and Libby. Even Newt had to blink them back.

The group moved to the kitchen where stew from lunch was set on the stove to reheat.

"Where's…Where's Nina?" Sally asked. Her voice was weak and filled with fear.

"She's napping upstairs in her room," Libby said. "With the twins."

"Can I see her?"

"Of course, come with me." Libby took Sally's shaking hand and led her through the house and up the stairs. "Do you want to wake her?" Libby spoke in a whisper as they approached the room with three sleeping children.

"Could I?"

"It's up to you. She'll wake on her own in about half an hour. You could have eaten by then."

Sally's stomach growled. "I'll just look for now."

"She's in here." Libby opened the door and stepped

aside.

Sally entered and made a b-line to the bed Nina slept in. Shaky hands fluttered to her mouth. She stood looking for a long moment, then turned away and left the room. Libby closed the door.

"She's your daughter, isn't she?" Libby embraced the weeping woman. They went across the hall into Libby's bedroom.

Sally nodded. "I thought she'd died back at the cave. They made us leave them. Just left them to die. Seems like Boy did. He were real sick when we left."

"Yes, the children told us they were burying him when they were found." They were silent for a moment, then Libby said, "Let's go get you some of that stew. Nina will be wanting your attention when she wakes."

The other women were in the washroom cleansing their faces and hands. Chloe was fluttering around. She couldn't stop hugging them.

"Dunc was so glad to meet Boone, Mae, and Tadpole again. Tadpole didn't remember him, but the others did." Chloe went on chattering about how delighted she was that the women had escaped and found their way to Stones Creek. "Only God could have brought you here. First the children, then you all got away. I just wish it could have been sooner."

"Stew's ready," Ruth said from the doorway. "Newt left. Said he'd come back later. He has some questions he wants to ask. Maybe you can help him locate the gang's camp."

When the three women were eating at a large table in the dining room with the Ladies and children gathered close by, Blanche said, "We're heating water for baths. We'll find clean clothes for you to wear and figure out which rooms you want as yours. That will be enough for today. The rest will be settled and explained tomorrow. Just know, you have a place here. This is Sanctuary House. You're safe and very welcome."

"But why?" Flora asked. "Why would you want us?"

Chloe explained about Sanctuary Place, the women's mission in Iowa where she, Duncan, and new born Lil-Pen were taken by Nugget Nate Ryder after he and Penny, his wife, found them in the shack in Minnesota. The Place was for women in need, whether of their own making, or thrust upon them. It was a safe place to live, learn skills for living and about the Lord.

"What about Gema? She live here?" Flora asked.

"She did, but she's married now to the man who found her when you helped her escape."

"I'm glad, we're glad she's okay. Hated to just make her run without knowin' how to get help, but even dyin' in the woods is a might better than what they'd planned for her." Flora spooned another bite of stew into her mouth.

Feet hitting the floor in the room above sounded. "That'll be Nina," Libby smiled. "She's got a heavy step for such a little thing. You want to come with me or wait until I bring her down?"

The footsteps ran across the floor above toward the stairs.

"No need to go, Sally. She'll be down in a few seconds," Ruth laughed.

Sally stood slowly and moved toward the door. Nina

came running in and stopped. Her eyes got big. "Mama." The word was whispered first, then shouted. Then, she was in her mother's arms. All Nina could say was, "Mama, Mama, Mama."

"My baby, my Nina," was repeated as they greeted each other.

Again tears flowed.

When everything settled again, Sally sat back down at the table with Nina on her lap. The little girl had a piece of bread and butter. When she'd finished eating, Nina placed buttery hands on Sally's cheeks.

"I no want to go back, Mama. Want to stay here. I gots a bed and lots to eat. Pretty dress."

Sally kissed Nina. "I don't want to go back either. I want to stay here, too."

~~~~~

Chloe sat with Flora on the porch swing of Sanctuary House. The women had bathed and were in borrowed clothing. None of it fit well since they were so very thin. The women didn't care. They were clean and not ragged.

"I still can't believe how you was found at that cabin we left you at. I was sure you'd die, and then Dunc would. When Buster told that he'd seen you in Stones Creek, I nearly dropped my teeth. Said he was going to get you back. That you belonged to them." She laughed. "I was glad to hear they got captured instead. It gave me hope I could get out. Me and the others talked about tryin'. It bein' winter, we couldn't even try. Had to wait until we could handle bein' out at least one night. Had to concern ourselves about the children, too.

"We was just about to gather what we needed and steal away when the sickness started. Roda died first. She was real sickly after that last baby were born. My two died, then Prue. Ada took it real hard. Prue'd been trying to protect Ada. Didn't do no good, but she tried. All the children took sick. I didn't, neither did Sally. We tended them all. Fred died. So did Clem. Men were getting fewer. We thought we'd be able to get away as soon as the weather turned."

"Then the men kidnapped Gema," Chloe said.

"Yeah, them idiots." Flora chuckled. "Picked the one town in the area with a sheriff who has some sense."

"Gema said you helped her escape."

"Yep, I told her I was gonna get them drunk, and she needed to run. Hear tell she did."

Chloe nodded. She knew what else had kept the men occupied so Gema could get away. "Red found her. They were stuck in the line shack on Hawk's Wing Ranch for several days. They got married about a week after they got back to town."

"The men were real mad about her gettin' away. Beat me up pretty bad. I wouldn't let them hurt Sally. It were my idea. They got real nervous after that. Knew the law would be comin'. Snow kept us at the cave for several days." Flora wiped her hand down her face. "When the snow melted, Ornan and Phil decided it was time to leave. They wouldn't take the children. Said they'd slow us down. They wanted Boone to come but not the others. He hid. I don't know where, don't care. He'd been wanting to escape, too. I tried to get them to leave Ada behind, but they wouldn't. Cletus said with two of the women dead, she needed to go along.

At least they left Mae.

"I were hopin' they were mad enough at me to leave me with the children. I was pretty beat up still. I pleaded with 'em, but they just threw me onto a horse with Ornan, and we rode away."

"God watched over them, Flora. Boone said they'd been alone at the cave for three days when the posse came. They were burying a little boy." Chloe put an arm around Flora's shoulders.

"Don't know nothin' about God watchin', but I'm glad they was found."

"I've no doubt God had His hand in all of this. God has turned what the gang meant for evil into good."

"How?" Flora asked.

"They kidnapped Gema, which was an evil thing to do. You helped her escape. That led to the children being rescued. Then, He had the gang set up camp where you could hear the trains. That gave you a way to get away and find Stones Creek. The town where the children are. Sally and Nina are back together. So are Ada and Boone. That should help both of them deal with their mother's death."

Flora nodded.

"Sheriff Riverby said he'd be telegraphing Nugget Nate. He's the sponsor of Sanctuary Place and House. I'm sure he'll help you get started in a new life."

"You think so?" Flora turned hope-filled eyes toward Chloe.

"He did for me. Nugget Nate and God."

~~~~~

Noah pulled the buggy to a halt in front of the main

house on Hawk's Wing Ranch. Ozzie jumped from his horse and tied his and the buggy horse to the hitching rail while Noah helped Blanche down. It was two days after the women had shown up in town. Yesterday, a posse had searched for the gang, having gotten general descriptions and landmarks from the women who'd escaped and come to Stones Creek.

The camp was found, but the men and all the supplies were gone. None of the posse had been surprised. With the women having escaped, the outlaws needed to vacate the area, knowing the law would be coming soon.

Hawk came out of the house, followed by Red. Noah noticed Hawk's gaze take in Blanche for a long moment. "Greetings, what brings you to Hawk's Wing this morning?" the ranch owner asked.

"We've got some news and wanted to let you know about it." Noah shifted his gaze to Red. "It concerns Gema. It's why Mrs. Basking is along."

Red looked at Hawk, then walked to the end of the long porch that stretched the length of the house and went down the steps, heading to his house.

"Let's mosey inside. I'll have Juanita get you something cool to drink. Morning, Mrs. Basking, Ozzie. Welcome to Hawk's Wing, or should I say welcome back?" Hawk ruffled Ozzie's hair after knocking his hat forward off his head.

Ozzie had been to the ranch several times. The first had been without permission. Ozzie was exercising one of the livery horses and had gone all the way to Hawk's Wing Ranch. It had been nearly dark when he got there and had begun to rain. Hawk put him up for the night and escorted him back to town early the next morning to his frantically worrying mother. That had been back in March, shortly before Gema was kidnapped.

Hawk and Blanche had talked. Ozzie was allowed to go to the ranch a couple of times a month, but only with his mother's and the livery owner's permission. Ozzie was working there after school and on Saturdays when needed.

Juanita had just served tea when Red and Gema entered. Gema went straight to Blanche, giving her a hug. "Very glad to see you, but why come?"

Blanche drew Gema to sit beside her on the settee. Red stood close by. "Gema, sweetie, the women who helped you get away from that outlaw gang. They've come to Stones Creek. They escaped."

Gema's mouth dropped open. "They okay? Safe?"

"Yes, very glad to be reunited with the children. They are living at the House. We're not sure how things will proceed. We've sent a telegram to Nate."

"Noah, why'd you feel it necessary to come clear out here to tell us that?" Red asked. "We'll be in town on Sunday. That's just a couple days away."

"We wanted you to know. We tracked back to their camp yesterday. It was on the far end of the Chasing R Ranch. They'd abandoned the camp. We know they're still in the area. Now, they don't have any women."

Gema paled. She jumped to her feet and clung to Red. She was trembling. Red wrapped his arms around her, holding her tightly to him. He looked at Hawk.

"Red, I want you and Gema to move into the main house for a while. Both women will be safer here, together,"

Hawk said. "I'll set a cowboy to be with them when you, I, or Alberto can't be here. They'll not be left alone." He walked over to Gema and touched her shoulder. "We'll keep you safe, Gema. You and Juanita."

~~~~~

Red followed Gema to the house. They were going to get clothing and other things they wanted to have at the main house. Gema stood in the middle of the kitchen, twisting her apron in her fists.

Red came up behind her and gripped her shoulders. "Don't fret. We'll keep you safe. I'll keep you safe."

"How? You gone much. I stole from street in middle of day."

"I'll arrange with Hawk that neither of you women will ever be alone. You'll not cross the yard alone."

"Those men mean. Hit woman, Flora. Leave children to die. They evil."

Red could feel her fear. She was trembling. Turning her, he pulled her into an embrace. "I won't let them take you again. You're my wife. I'll see you safe. Trust me."

She collapsed against him, weeping out her fear. When she quieted, Gema tilted her head back and studied him. "I trust."

"Let's gather what we want to take. Don't worry about taking everything you might need. We can come back for anything else." He grinned at her. "It's not like it's that far."

Gema gave a weak smile, stepped away and went into the bedroom. When she had her canvas bag filled, Gema asked, "I take my music? Hawk let me practice in house?"

"More likely you need Juanita's permission. I think she pretty much rules the roost."

"Roost?"

"House. She's more boss of the house than Hawk is. He may think he is. Men may be king of the castle, but women are the queens of the house."

Gema still looked confused.

"Just ask Juanita if it's okay with her if you play. I'm sure she'll approve." Red waited until she'd gathered her music, then he picked up her bag and his. Gema held the bundle of papers as they walked back to the main house.

CHAPTER ELEVEN

NEWT AND Dak were discussing the next scouting party they were sending out hunting for the King Gang. At least that was what he thought they were still calling themselves. The King brothers had been captured when they came to town last December, trying to take Chloe back to the gang.

Cowboys on all the ranches were on the lookout as they rode the range. Newt thought they might have left the area, but Flora just kept saying they were idiots and stupid. She figured they weren't smart enough to head to some other part of the territory. She seemed to know since she'd been with them for many years. Newt would continue the search. Maybe they were stupid enough to stick around.

The westbound train pulled into the station, emitting its loud whistle as it approached and came to a stop with a clattering and a whoosh of steam. Newt stopped speaking until the noise subsided. He poured himself and Dak a fresh cup of coffee. No sense in taking up the conversation again just yet. In a few minutes, it would pull out again with the rattle and whistle, making speech impossible until it was out of town.

When he heard the switch engine bellow, Newt glanced out the window. A green and gold Pullman car with a cattle car behind were being moved onto the side track. There was only one couple who had a Pullman car that Newt knew of, Nugget Nate and Penny Ryder.

What were they doing back in town? A telegram telling of the women escaping the gang and coming to town had only been sent a day or two ago.

Ben Cutler, who owned the general store, hadn't said anything about his uncle coming to town. It was a year and a half since they had visited. They'd arrived while the town was in crisis with the kidnapping of Doc Eli Steele and Leah Daniels. Nate had shown up, saying he'd had a Callin' to come to Stones Creek. He'd done in a few hours what the rest of the men hadn't been able to do in several days of searching, find where Eli and Leah were trapped in a cave.

Had Nate had another of his Callin's? Was he here to help find the outlaws? Only one way to find out. Newt set his coffee cup on his desk, grabbed his hat, and headed out the door.

Several other townsfolk had seen the Pullman car being side tracked. Ben was jumping down from the boardwalk in front of his store. Eli was in the street, walking toward the train station, as were McIlroy and Noah.

The tall mountain man leaped from the rear porch of the Pullman, but ignored the men. He headed to the cattle car, opened the door and climbed in, disappearing into its darkness.

A thin man with a stiff bearing came out of the car and

placed a set of stairs on the platform. Behind him an auburn-haired woman dressed in an olive green travel suit allowed him to help her descend. She crossed the platform and stopped. Surveying the crowd of people now filling the street, she smiled and waved.

"Ben," she called. "Come greet your Aunt Penny."

Ben ran to the station and hugged Penny, swinging her down from the platform onto the street.

"Aunt Penny, what are you and Uncle Nate doing here? You didn't write and let us know you were coming."

"You know your Uncle Nate. He gets a Calling, and nothing will stop him. We have to go right now, no delay. Fortunately, I keep the Pullman stocked with clothing and food."

"How are Sarah and the children? They've probably grown several inches since we've seen them."

"They are doing well. Sarah's a bit under the weather." At Penny's look of concern, Ben said, "Nothing a few months won't fix."

"Penny, m' love. You's can be a catchin' up on the family oncest I get the low down on why I's needed here again." Nate led a white horse to a water trough in front of the jail. "There ya be, Lightnin'. Drink yer fill."

Nate looked around. When his eyes lit on Newt, he finished tying Lightning's reins to the rail. "So, Sheriff, what be troublin' here in Stones Creek that be needin' my skills?"

"How'd you get here so quickly? I just sent the telegram day before yesterday. We didn't expect you to come. Just let us know what to do about the women."

"I got me a Callin' 'bout a week ago. Took a few days ta

make all the switchin' ta get pulled ta here. Mighty sorrowful fer the delay."

"What women, Sheriff?" Penny was now standing beside her husband who'd placed an arm around her waist.

"How about we go to the jail, and I'll explain it all?"

~~~~~

"That's just about everything," Newt said. He was leaning against the wall, his arms across his chest. Penny was seated at his desk. Nate was pacing from inside a cell to the stove and back. "Can you think of anything else, Dak?"

"Other than all the women are scared of being kidnapped, I'd say you covered it pretty well." Dak was sitting on the floor with his legs stretched out in front of him. "Cora doesn't want to leave the flat. She'll take Susan over to the House to visit with the Ladies since she can just cross the alley, but she won't even go to the general store alone."

"You married one of the House Ladies, didn't you, Deputy?" Penny asked.

"Yes, ma'am. I'm going to be adopting Susan as soon as Four gets all the paperwork done. Newt's adopting Troy, Myra's son, too." Dak nodded at his boss.

"Four?" Penny asked.

"He's the new lawyer in town. He has an office in the bank. His name's Forsyth Franklin Fredrick Farnsworth the Fourth," Newt explained. "We just call him Four."

Nate let out a howl of laughter. "With a name as cornvulutioned as that, I'd be a thinkin' of somethin' else ta be called, too." He sobered. "Nowst, I'm a gonna be wantin' ta jaw a bit within' the women whatst done escaped them no-count varnmints. Needs ta be gittin' acquaintioned up wit' them anyways."

"Yes," Penny said. "Maybe they will allow us to escort them to Iowa, to Sanctuary Place. They will need time to adjust to polite society, learn skills, etc."

"Polite society, woman, where does ya come up with that high falutin' talk? They's bein' needin' ta learn howst ta live amongst reg'lar, law 'bidin', God fearin' peoples. They's sure ta be needin' ta learn 'bout the love God's a got for 'em." Nate now stood next to Penny's chair, looking down at her with his hands on his hips.

Penny reached up and patted her husband on the cheek. "Yes, dear."

~~~~~

"Nate, promise me you'll just scout. If you find them…"

"When I finds 'em. Ain't no iffen 'bout it." Nate interrupted Newt. They were standing nose to nose. Penny's eyes were twinkling with mirth, as were Dak's. The sheriff and the mountain man had been arguing about how to find and apprehend the criminal gang.

"When you find them," Newt sighed. "You promise me you'll come back so we can gather up the posse. I don't want you trying to capture them all by yourself."

"I was trained up by Davy Crockett, hisself," Nate began.

Newt held up his hand, stopping the flood of protest he knew was coming. "I know. You're very talented and capable. You could probably fight off every outlaw in the territory at the same time with one hand tied behind your back. You need to let us mere men have a hand in this.

"These outlaws have harmed our women, abandoned children to die, robbed stages, banks, and murdered innocent people. The men of Stones Creek want to have a hand in bringing them to justice. Are you going to deny them that?"

Nate deflated. "You's right, Sheriff. I were bein' plumb selfish. A wantin' all the glory myself. Not atall how's a believin' man should be a actin'. The men o' Stones Creek need ta be a feelin' they was a part o' this. Ev'n though we's all know I could a done it myself."

"Besides," Penny said, quietly. "All the glory belongs to the Almighty anyway."

Nate went to his wife and kissed her. "You's hit the nail square on the head, m' love. God be the one what called us ta Stones Creek, and He be's the One what'll round up 'em varnmints so's they can spend the rest o' their days in the hoosegow."

"So," Newt tried to take control of the meeting again. "You, Nate, will go scout until you find where the gang is. Then, you'll come back, and we'll gather the posse to go after them. I've got five town men, not counting Dak and me. I know Hawk and Red want to be involved, as do Linc, Wes, and Spike from the Chasing R. Cowboys from both those ranches and some others are willing too, if there's time to contact them. Some I'll keep in town, just in case."

"Oh's kay. I'll be headin' out in the mornin' an' rustle me up a bunch o' outlaws ta be captured." Nate grabbed Penny's hand hauling her to her feet. "Come on, Penny, m' love. We's got some great-nephews and a great-niece we ain't seed in nie on two years. I got me a hankerin' to spread out some hugs an' kisses."

~~~~~

Gema woke with a start. Red had jumped out of bed and was pulling his pants on. It was night, but moonlight dimly illuminated their room. The chickens were squawking loudly, and the roosters were crowing. They were agitated. Angry. The pigs were squealing.

"What goes?" Gema clutched the covers to her chest.

"Something's in the chicken house. Could be a coyote. Maybe a fox or wolf. Don't fret. I'll be back shortly. Just don't go near the window." Red shoved his feet into his boots, grabbed his revolver and ran out the door.

Gema could hear others running down the stairs, too. Hawk and Alberto. Shouts came from the bunkhouse. Then, the sound of horses galloping away. She got up and went into the hall. Juanita was there. They hugged each other. That was a universal language.

When the shouting and running stopped, Juanita pulled back. "Come. Make coffee. Men," she said a spate of words in Spanish. Gema grabbed a shawl and wrapped it around her shoulders. She followed Juanita to the kitchen and was set to slicing bread while the housekeeper stirred up the coals and made coffee.

Just as it began to boil, the men came in through the mudroom.

"Looks like they got about six chickens," Hawk said. "Maybe one was a rooster. The birds were so flustered and running around, it was hard to tell."

"I think they got that ornery rooster. I didn't see him

out there," Alberto said. "He'll peck them. Maybe take his spurs to them. Serve them right if he does."

Red went to where Gema was still slicing bread. She'd sliced two loaves already and was starting on a third. He stopped her hand and took the knife from her, setting it on the table beside the piles of bread slices. "Are you okay?"

She turned wide frightened eyes to him and dove against his chest. Her arms wrapped around his waist, and she hung on as if she were drowning. "So scared. For you. For me. Thanking God for protection."

"Who steal los pollos?" Juanita asked.

"There were three of them. I'm thinking they may be from the King Gang. We've been fortunate so far that we haven't had anything stolen before."

Gema began trembling in Red's arms. "I'm going to skip the coffee. Thank you, Juanita, for thinking of it. Gema and I will see you in the morning." He glanced at the clock on a shelf above the stove. "I guess it is morning, but I don't have to get up for another hour. See you then."

Placing his hand on Gema's back, he guided her from the room and up the stairs. He tucked her into bed, then got in on his side. She rolled toward him. Red wrapped his arms around her, holding her against his chest, her head tucked under his chin. Running his fingers across her cheek, he tucked a lock of hair that had come loose from her braid behind Gema's ear.

"You're safe, Gema. I'll not let anyone take you from me."

"Truly?" The word was whispered against his chest.

"Truly. I'll always protect you."

She sighed and relaxed against him. "You will. I know. I trust."

~~~~~

Nate stood on the front porch of his Pullman rail car. Steam rose from the morning dew sprinkled on the grass by the tracks. He lifted his eyes to heaven. "Lord, ya done brought me an' Penny here. We done followed yer Callin'. Obeyin' as quick like as we's could. I'm a askin' fer yer help now. Yer Word says ya be callin' for justice. 'At we should be a fightin' evil. Well, evil been done 'round these parts. A good man been murdered. His wife dyin' from her grief, as well as the measles, leavin' two babes orphaned. Ya know what they done ta Chloe an' Dunc. Ya done rescued them nie on six years ago.

"Now, ya done got them young'uns and them women outa the clutches of them evil men. I be a thankin' ya greatly fer that. Ya done that so's ta set up my comin' so's ya can show me where's they be a hidin'. I's askin' ya ta do that now, Lord. Guide me ta where the varnmints is hangin' out. I'm askin' in His name. Amen."

Nate jumped to the ground and strode to the livery where Lightning had spent the night. The horse was eager to get underway. He always was when they followed a Calling. He seemed to get them, too. If Nate was unsure which way to go, he trusted Lightning to head in the right direction.

This morning, though, Nate knew he had to head west. If asked, he wouldn't be able to explain why. He'd just say that was the direction he needed to go.

Nate rode along the railroad tracks. The ground sloped

up toward the mountains. The forest thickened. He saw several deer and wished he had time to hunt. He could use a new set of buckskins. Penny was harping at him about it. Said his were getting too dirty to even try to come clean.

An invisible tug made him turn south. He sniffed the air. Could he smell wood smoke? He gave Lightning his head, and they quietly moved through the trees. The scent of burning wood became stronger.

Nate dismounted and tied Lightning to a branch. He pulled his new repeating rifle from the saddle boot. He wasn't going to try and take them, but he'd be prepared in case they spotted him.

Moving silently through the forest, Nate surveyed the landscape. There looked to be a cliff ahead. He was on the top. The land dropped away suddenly. He lay on his belly and crawled to the edge. Voices argued below him.

"I says we need to head out of here. This place ain't been that good to us. First, Buster an' Amos try ta get Chloe back and get themselves captured. Then, the sickness comes. Prue and Roda dies up on us. Some of them kids, too."

Another voice chimed in. "Yeah, then you goes an' takes that foreign girl. The one what can't speak English. She escapes."

"Flora made that happen," A third disgruntled voice said.

"Still, she got away," the first man said. "I'm not thinkin' you're a very good leader, Ornan. I'm thinking it might be time for someone else to call the shots."

"Just you wait a minute, Phil." Ornan spent some time

turning the air blue with his words. "I'm still leader here, and what I say goes."

"We'll just see about that when Dudley, Stew, and Cletus get back. They was headed to some ranch to pick up a couple of chickens. Left last night. Should be back soon. We can all discuss who's going to be leadin' the gang now, and what we do next. I say it won't be you."

Nate heard the sound of a fist hitting flesh as he backward crawled from the edge. He needed to exit fast if three of the outlaws were returning.

When he reached Lightning, Nate shoved the rifle into its boot, untied the reins, mounted, and hightailed it back to town. If he was fast enough, maybe the posse could return before nightfall and capture the gang today. By the sounds of their discussion, it might not be long before a new leader had them vacating the area heading for better luck in their dastardly deeds.

Nate thanked the Lord as he rode that he'd found the camp so quickly. The way the land lay, the posse should be able to get the drop on them from several directions. The cover was good to protect themselves if shooting began.

Two men were riding toward Nate along the tracks. They didn't veer off when they saw him, so Nate figured they weren't part of the gang. As he approached, he recognized one of the men. It was Spike Hunter from the Chasing R Ranch. Spike raised a hand and waved.

"Nugget Nate Ryder, you ole coot, you. What are you doing in these parts?" Spike asked when they drew near.

"Had me a Callin' so Penny an' me, we done come back. Got in yesterday. Been out scoutin' them varmints what have been tormentin' the area. Found 'em. We's needin' ta get up the posse real quick like. They's may be a fixin' ta vamoose. They be a argufyin' about who's the biggest toad in the puddle."

Spike turned to the other man. "Jeb, you head back to Hawk's Wing. I'll go to the Chasing R." He looked at Nate. "We'll get our men and meet you at the jail as soon as we can. Maybe we'll be able to grab them up today."

Jeb took off one direction and Spike the other. Nate continued to town, once again thanking the One in control for His providence.

~~~~~

"Gema," Red called as he ran into the main house. Jeb had come back to the homestead saying Nugget Nate Ryder had found the King Gang's hideout. They were getting up a posse and wanted as many men as wanted to go. Hawk had set Alberto to picking which cowboys would be the most help to the posse and the others to continue with their duties. Red hadn't waited for instructions. He'd just run to the house.

He'd promised early that morning that he would always protect Gema, and he was going to keep his word. Rather than leave her on the ranch, he was going to take her to Stones Creek. She could stay at the House with the other Ladies. There would be men in town keeping it safe while the posse hunted the outlaws.

Hank. The name of his best friend came to Red's mind. Yes, Hank would keep the Ladies safe. He was married to one, after all, Laura. Her rejection led Red to the line shack on the end of Hawk's Wing Ranch, where he found Gema running from the outlaws who had kidnapped her.

Red was sure Hank would be staying in town rather than going with the posse. He didn't like riding and wasn't that great with a gun. Hank and Red had both been hired on as cowboys when they came west after the war. Hank didn't like the work and had gone to Denver to learn barbering. He'd come to Stones Creek and set up his barber shop and bathing house. There was no one Red trusted more to protect the woman he loved than Hank Johnson.

Red nearly missed a step as he ran up the stairs when the realization hit him. He loved Gema. The thought stopped him half way to the second floor. Loved her more than life itself. If anything happened to her, he would be devastated. She'd become the focus of all he did and hoped to achieve. When had that happened? He hadn't a clue and didn't have time to think about it now. He had to get her to town.

Violin music coming from their bedroom made his feet move again. They needed to get to town. Red was going to go with that posse to apprehend the men who had kidnapped Gema with evil intentions. None of them was going to escape justice. He'd see to that.

The music stopped as Red ran down the hall. Gema must have heard him coming. The door opened before he took hold of the knob.

"What wrong, Red? Why run?"

"Nugget Nate found where the King Gang is. They're getting up a posse. Hawk and I are going, along with several cowboys."

Gema gasped.

"Gema, I want to take you to town. To the House. You'll feel safer there with your friends. I'll feel better knowing you're there. I won't worry if we miss the gang that you're here."

"Juanita?" She set the violin and bow on the washstand.

"Alberto and about half the cowboys will be here. They'll keep her safe. It's you I'm concerned with. You'll be much more at ease being in town. Pack a bag just in case it's too late to come back to the ranch tonight. I'm going to saddle Ralph. Meet me downstairs as soon as you're ready." Red gave her a quick kiss and left.

When he got to the stable, Ralph, as well as another of the cow ponies, were waiting. Cookie held the reins.

"You and Gema ride on Blackie. That'll keep Ralph fresh for when you head out with the posse."

"Good thinking. Thanks. How'd you know I was taking Gema to town?"

"Figured you'd want her there, just in case you don't come back."

"You're smarter than you look. I didn't tell her that, but it's one reason I'm taking her. The other is, I think she'll feel safer with her friends. I know she'd be safe here, but she needs the support the Ladies can give her."

Cookie nodded while Red mounted Blackie. The cowboys who were going to town were mounting, too. Hawk came from the stable leading Pecos, a brown stock horse he'd purchased from Lucy Tanner after her husband had been murdered by the King Gang.

"You ready, Red?" Hawk asked.

"Yeah, just have to get Gema." Red kicked Blackie,

turning the horse toward the house. Gema was coming out the front door, her carpet bag in her hand. Juanita followed, wringing her hands and chattering in Spanish. Alberto jogged over, spoke to her, and gave her a hug.

"Ready to go," Gema said. A cowboy took the bag from her and tied it to the back of Blackie's saddle. Alberto boosted her up in front of Red.

"Vàmonos," Hawk called. He, Red, and four cowboys took off at a gallop headed for Stones Creek. Jeb held Ralph's lead rein. Gema tucked herself against Red who wrapped his arm around her waist.

CHAPTER TWELVE

"PRAY," NOAH said to his wife, Vernie. "That's the best thing you can do. I'm hoping we'll find them and have an easy time bringing them in." He buckled his twin holster belt and tied the thongs around his legs. Slipping his arms into the sleeves of his black duster coat, Noah put his black wide-brimmed hat on. "You head over to Almeda and Thomas' soddy. You both will be safe there."

After kissing Vernie and one-year-old Dottie, he took one last look and left the apartment. He had a couple of stops to make before he went to the jail to join the posse.

First, Pastor Preston went to his gun shop and filled a sack with bullet boxes. He'd supply the posse with whatever they needed in the way of ammunition. He took a moment to check both of his Colt Army Revolvers, making sure they were fully loaded with six bullets each.

As much as he hated violence, Noah knew there were times when it was necessary to stop evil from perpetuating itself. Twenty years ago, he hadn't been old enough to stop his sister, Chloe, from being kidnapped while their father held to his non-violent belief and stood like a statue allowing it to happen. Years of Noah's prayers had been answered when Chloe Ashburn had come to Stones Creek with the Ladies of Sanctuary House. His beloved older sister was restored to him.

Now, Noah had the chance to bring the outlaw gang to account for their actions. He planned to do just that. While he filled his gun belt loops with bullets, Noah prayed his motive would be pure, in alignment with God's desire for justice. Deep in Noah's soul was a longing for vengeance. "Keep me from acting on this longing, Lord. Still my hand if my actions slip from doing your will."

Locking the shop, Noah went next door to Johnson's Barber Shop and Bath house. Hank and Laura were inside.

"Pastor," Hank said.

"Hank, Laura. I'm heading out with the posse. Most of the men of town are. You've still got a Colt Army, don't you?"

"Yes."

"Here." Noah placed a box of .44 caliber bullets on the counter. "I don't know who all Sheriff Riverby will have stay to protect the town, but I'm hoping you'll be one to help protect the Ladies."

"Laura and I were just talking about that. We're going to take the boys and go over to the House. I'll stay there with them until the posse comes back. Davis was in earlier. He's making sure all the horses at his livery are ready to go, but he's staying in town, too."

"Good."

"Homer Fugard and Bufford Brook are staying too."

Noah snorted. "Not much protection there. Thomas is

staying in town with Almeda and the baby. Vernie and Dottie are going to stay with them in the soddy."

The back door to the shop opened, and Red Dickerson entered. He had the holsters tied down on his thighs, too. "Hank, Laura, Pastor." Red nodded to each. "Hank, I just left Gema at the House. I'd be appreciative if you'd head over there and stay with the Ladies…"

"Already planning to, Red. Noah and I were just talking about who's staying in town."

Red looked at Laura. "If anything happens, I'd like you to see Gema through it, Laura. She trusts you. I think she misses you most of all the Ladies."

Laura took Red's hand. "You know I would, but it's not going to be necessary. We're going to spend the time lifting you all up to the Lord for protection and success."

"We'll take all the prayers you have."

"I'm going to get the boys now," Laura said, releasing Red's hand. "I'll meet you at the House."

The men watched her leave.

"Let's get to the jail, Red," Noah said.

Red nodded. "Thanks, Hank. I appreciate your help."

"Anytime, my friend. Anytime."

~~~~~

Red and Noah strode down the street. A group of men stood in front of the jail, waiting to mount up. Red knew them all. Was friends with them. Would they all still be alive after today?

"Red," Ben Cutler called as he crossed from his general store to where the posse was gathering.

"I'm going inside to let them know we've arrived," Noah said.

"What can I do for you, Ben?" Red asked.

"I just wanted to tell you the order you placed a while back arrived. You can get it when we get back." Ben clapped a hand on Red's shoulder.

"Thanks. I will." Red paused. "Ben, if something happens, you'll give it to Gema, won't you? And see that she's settled back at the House? She'll need to be with the Ladies."

"Don't talk like that, Red. We're going to roust out the King Gang."

"Promise me, Ben. I need to know she'll be taken care of."

"You know I will. We all will, but it won't be necessary. Justice will prevail. We'll rid Colorado of the King Gang once and for all," Ben said. Then he winked. "How can it go any other way? My Uncle Nugget Nate Ryder always gets what he's after. Well, so long as Aunt Penny approves, that is."

~~~~~

"Dak, you set the cowboys around town. I'm leaving you and Spike in charge here. Make sure Fugard and Brook stay in their houses. I don't want them waving firearms around. They're liable to accidentally shoot something or somebody. Thomas has his rifle. Davis will stay at his livery."

Noah entered. "Hank has a Colt Army. I gave him a box of bullets. He's going to be at the House."

"I'm setting Four there, too," said Newt. "He's got

experience from the War."

Dak and Newt finished discussing where to post the cowboys around town. Noah made sure each of the posse members, as well as those staying in town, had enough ammunition.

"You's about done jawin', Sheriff? I'm a thinkin' we's a needin' ta be headin' out. We's burnin' daylight." Nugget Nate straightened from leaning against the jail wall.

"Yeah, Nate. I think we've covered everything."

They exited the jail and mounted. Dak and Spike spoke with the cowboys who were staying in town. Newt looked over his town. They were heading out to hopefully make the area safer for the townsfolk and those living on ranches and farms in the area.

"Hey, Nate," Linc Pierce, foreman of the Chasing R Ranch and son-in-law to Wes Chase, the owner, called. "I see you have a new repeating rifle. What happened to old Betsy?"

Nate grunted. "Old Betsy's fine. Better 'an this new-fangled one. But it do let me plug them varnmints quicker."

The rest of the posse laughed.

Noah led the men in prayer, lifting up thanks that Nate was able to find the camp so quickly. Then, he asked for calm minds and steady hands as the posse went to track them down.

"You lead the way, Nate," Newt said. "We'll follow in pairs."

Nate kicked Lightning into a gallop and headed west along the railroad tracks. When he got to the place he'd entered the woods, Nate halted and looked back at the men following.

"Somethin' ain't right. Don't rightly know what, jes know."

"How do you want to proceed?" Newt asked.

"I'd say, go on to the camp, but be warier 'an a rabbit 'mongst a den o' foxes."

The rest of the men followed Nate into the trees. He stopped and dismounted where he had before. From there, they spread out and continued on foot. As they neared the top of the cliff, they saw a small figure standing facing them. It was a woman wrapped in a large shawl even though the June day was warm.

"That's Wise One. She's an old Indian woman who lives in the forest on the Chasing R," Linc said. "Norie gave her that shawl. Come on. Let's go talk to her."

Linc, Newt, and Nate walked up to the Indian.

"You not find them here. The evil ones head that way. Go by where I pick berries. Say they go to town to rob bank and get women. Say they shoot town up. Show who big man. I come here. Tell you."

"They's headed ta Stones Creek. That be what the Callin' was tryin' ta tell me back at the track. Let's ride." Nate was already running toward where they'd tied the horses as he yelled.

CHAPTER THIRTEEN

"WILL YOU please quit pacing? You're making us all nervous," Laura said. "Especially, the children." The last was whispered as Laura took Gema by the arm and led her into her old bedroom. "All your worrying is only going to wear you out and get the babies upset. I never thought the House could ever be crowded, but with twenty-seven women and children on the top two floors at the back of the house, it is."

Hank wanted the Ladies and children off the first floor and in the rooms to the rear of the building. There was less likelihood of a stray bullet aimed at the house hitting anyone.

Blanche had protested the restriction. "Do you really think the gang will come to town? I thought Nate found them, and the posse was going to go capture them."

"Well, ma'am. It's better to be safe than sorry. That bunch of no-accounts don't have respect or caring for any living thing but themselves. If they've gotten any type of notion there's a posse coming after them, it's mighty likely they'll be hot-footing it to town with evil intent." Hank stood in the dining room where everyone had gathered. The married Ladies whose husbands were in the posse or guarding the town had come to the House to wait together. "I'd feel a might more at ease if you all would just mosey upstairs and arrange yourselves like I suggested."

Blanche studied Hank for a long moment. "All right, we will. First, though, I want to prepare some food for when the men return. Enough for the posse and the men guarding around town."

Chloe McIlroy stood. "I'll get pans from the café. They'll be big enough. What are you thinking we should make?"

"Macaroni, cheese pudding with ham, cornbread, and I think Almeda baked a couple of cakes this morning. I'll check and see if they are still in the bakery." Blanche headed to the kitchen. Chloe, along with several other Ladies followed, crossing the alley between the House and the back of the Creek Café. If they were going to be preparing enough food for all the men, they'd need help, both in the fixing and gathering of ingredients.

Now, everyone was upstairs. The baking dishes were waiting to go into the oven. The cornbread would be mixed up when the men came back to town. They would also serve pickles the Ladies had put up last summer and, of course, plenty of coffee.

Gema paced from the door to the window over and over while Laura looked on.

"Come, sit, Gema," Laura said, sitting on the bed.

Gema sat beside her. "I'm so scared. What if Red not come back? What would I do?"

"Why do you think he won't come back?" Laura placed her arm around the younger woman's shoulders.

"Those men. They very bad. Evil. They fight back at posse. Not want to be captured. Maybe shoot at posse. What if Red…" Gema bit on her knuckle.

"Are you scared for you or for Red?"

"Both. Want Red safe. Want stay Red's wife."

"Red's a good man, isn't he?" Laura smiled.

"Yes, very good man." Gema giggled. "When he find me. So very careful. Help me get out of wet clothes. Careful to no look. So funny. Not see at time. Too cold and wet. Now, see how funny." She covered her mouth with her fingers and giggled some more. When she stopped, Gema looked at Laura, a soft smile on her face. "He give me back my music."

"Your music?"

"Let me play Jeb's violin." Gema explained about her father selling her instrument and the years she'd been unable to play. Red's restrictions on being with the cowboys and his allowing her to play. "Cowboy now very respectful. No make crude jokes. Like listen when I play. Red give music back to me."

Laura studied Gema. *"All things work to the good for those who love God, for those who are called according to his purpose.* Seems to me Red learned something about how to treat his woman since he and I were courting. If I had married Red, he wouldn't have been at the line shack when you were kidnapped. You could have died from exposure. Instead, Hank told me he loved me. Red rescued you, and now, you love him."

Gema's mouth dropped open. After a long moment of silence, she said, "You right. I do love Red. Not know until you say, but I do. Love him humungous lot."

The women hugged.

Shots could be heard sounding as if they were coming from Main Street. Eddie and Mark, Laura's sons, burst into the room, terror on their faces.

"Come on," Laura said, as she and Gema stood. "Under the bed just as Hank said." They shoved the trundle bed out of the way and crawled under, each lady with her arms wrapped around a small boy.

~~~~~

The posse was just outside of town when Newt held up his hand. The ten members of the posse stopped as he turned around.

"I want to split us up to come into town from all sides at once. Hawk, you, Red, and Linc circle around to the south and come in from behind the church. Wes, Noah, Massot, you come in from the west. Jeb, Eli, Ben, come in from behind Ben's store. I'm going to give you all five minutes to get in position."

Newt's instructions were cut off by the sound of gunfire. The posse spurred their mounts, taking off at a gallop. Newt spun his horse and did the same.

~~~~~

Red's heart was pounding nearly as loudly as Ralph's hooves were against the ground. Gema, his Gema was in town and so was the gang that had kidnapped her.

As they neared the station, several of the men went behind it, three others turned to head up Main Street. Red felt like he should follow, but everything in him said to go straight to Sanctuary House. That was where his wife was.

Hawk and Massot joined him as he rode behind the livery and stopped close to the back wall. They dismounted and shooed their horses back toward the railroad tracks. Gunfire could be heard coming from both the House and the woods near Massot's carpenter shop.

"There's one on your roof, Massot," Hawk said softly. "At least one in the woods." All three men pulled their revolvers from their holsters.

Red studied the building across the street from the House. It looked like only one man was taking cover behind the roof façade, but he'd be careful to keep a lookout for another. Turning his attention to the woods, Red saw a man lean out from behind a tree and shoot at the house. It seemed they hadn't been spotted next to the back of the general store.

Movement up the street caught Red's eye. A man was crossing and would be out of sight to the men in the building. He knew Hank was in there, but someone else was shooting, too. Maybe it was one of the Ladies, but Red didn't think so. At least he'd never heard that any could shoot.

He watched the man in the street work his way diagonally toward the House but not at an angle that would take him to the front. The outlaw was heading for the alley and the back door to the House.

"Look," Red pointed at the man. "He's going to the alley. There's a back way in. I'm going to get him before he does." He looked at Hawk who nodded.

"We'll cover you. We won't shoot unless one of them takes aim. We don't want to let them know we're here."

Red moved along the wall, watching between the man on the roof and the one he knew of in the woods. He stopped when the man on the roof fell over the façade, landing with a thud on the ground. One down. At least three more to go.

The smell of gunpowder stung his nose. The town seemed to be filled with smoke from all the shooting. There was a battle going on at the bank, too.

He'd reached the end of the building and needed to cross the street to go along the side of the House and on into the alley. That would draw attention to him. He waited until the next shots came from the House, darted around the corner, and up the street. A glance at the part of Main Street visible between the buildings revealed several bodies lying in the dust. He didn't know if they were dead or wounded.

Crossing to the other side, Red flattened himself against the building. He moved quickly to the corner and looked around. The outlaw was creeping up the steps. Red aimed and pulled the trigger. The outlaw dropped.

Red ran up the alley and kicked the gun lying next to the man away. Another round of shots was fired from the House. He heard more than two guns. He hoped it was Hawk and Massot getting into the fight. Leaning down, he flipped the man over. He was dead. Red felt no remorse. That surprised him, but he didn't have time to think about it now. He ran back to the street, stopping before he got to the end of the building. Peeking out, Massot running toward him startled Red.

"We've got all of them that we saw. Hawk's checking the woods. He wants us to help those on Main Street."

Red nodded. "Let's go this way." He ran back up the alley and opened the back door to Hank's barbershop. They might be able to get a drop on those in the street without revealing themselves. At least for a while.

They crept along the hall and ducked as they entered the front room. There was a large window, and Red didn't want to be seen before he was in place. He couldn't believe the glass was still intact. He crouched down. Massot did the same. They crawled to the window and peaked over the sill.

The street was empty but for several bodies. Red recognized a cowboy from Hawk's Wing. He hoped the man was only wounded. He couldn't tell from this distance.

"You better give up." It was Newt Riverby yelling from somewhere to the left. "You don't stand a chance. We've stopped the men trying to take the House. You won't get the women. You won't get away with any money either." Hawk must have gotten to the sheriff if he knew they'd taken out the men attacking the House.

"We'll take our chances." That voice Red didn't recognize. It came from his right. Were they holed up in the café? It was next door to where he and Massot were.

Several shots came from the hotel. Red didn't know who was in there. No way could he shoot. It might be part of the posse or those who stayed to guard the town.

"Come on," Red said in a hushed voice. He crawled back to the hall before he stood. "Let's head for the back door of the café. I think some of them might be in there."

"Sounded like that man was talking from there," Massot said.

Easing open the door, Red looked up and down the alley. It was clear. He waved Massot to follow. They crept to the door into the café, one on each side. He lifted the latch and gave it a gentle push, keeping his body shielded by the wall. It didn't squeak as it swung open. Both men looked in. They could see through the kitchen and into the dining room under the swinging doors which divided the two rooms.

Tables were turned on their sides, being used as more shielding than just the front wall gave. Two men crouched behind them. One man was yelling obscenities while the other was reloading his pistol. Red thought to take a moment to reload his gun, but he'd only taken one shot. He had five more. He glanced at Massot who was slipping bullets into their slots. When he finished, he nodded at Red.

Carefully, so as to not make a sound, Red stepped into the kitchen. He moved to the side so he couldn't be seen if one of the outlaws glanced back. Massot did the same. They crossed the kitchen. Massot moved to the pass-through window and settled himself, taking aim.

Red pushed one side of the swinging door open. A squeak had the outlaws spinning around. Four guns fired. Two outlaws dropped. A sting which grew into massive pain entered Red's left shoulder. He ducked into the kitchen and leaned against the wall, clutching his wound. Taking a deep breath, he glanced at Massot.

"I'm fine. We need to check those men."

Massot kept his position while Red went into the front

room. The place was in shambles. The outlaws had broken just about every chair and table. The large front window was shattered. Glass littered the floor.

Kicking the dropped guns away, Red checked both men. One was dead, the other probably would be soon from the looks of his gut shot. He was breathing heavily but not moving. The hate in his eyes indicated his lack of remorse for all he'd done.

"Was it all worth it?" Red asked, standing over the man. There was no reply. Red took the guns from the second holster on each man. Once that was done, Massot joined him in the dining room, keeping aim on the wounded man.

Red moved to the front wall, keeping from being exposed to the street. "We've got these two in the café, Newt," he yelled. "One's dead. The other will be shortly."

"Who's we?" Seems Newt wasn't taking any chances that an outlaw was smart enough to try and trick him.

"Red and Massot."

"Hear that?" Newt yelled. "Your numbers are getting mighty slim. Let's see, the four trying to take the House, three dead in the street, two in the café. That's nine. The count of the horses we know you rode in on only leaves two of you. Best give up now."

"Not gonna happen, Sher…" The word was cut off.

"Only one varnmint left now, Newt." It was Nugget Nate who called out.

"I give up. I give up." That voice sounded young. "Stop." The last word was fairly screamed.

"I's got me this'un, too." Again Nate called out. "But afore I's a comin' out inta the street, I be a thinkin' ya needs ta check all them bodies. Ain't of a mind ta get me shot up cause o' a miscountin'."

Red exchanged a grin with Massot. Nate might not have a decent command of grammar, but he didn't lack anything when it came to tactics.

CHAPTER FOURTEEN

RED STRAIGHTENED from leaning against the wall. Seems it was over now. He needed to see Gema. Needed to know she was all right. "I need to get to the House and find Gema."

"You better get that tended to first," Massot said. "You don't want her fainting on you."

Red looked down. His shirt and vest were covered in blood. He thought the bleeding may have stopped but wasn't positive. "You're probably right. Besides we need to talk with Newt."

"Yeah."

They checked on the wounded outlaw whose life was draining away into a bloody puddle on the floor. Massot picked up the guns, stuffing them into his belt. "Let's go. He's not going to be going anywhere soon. Well, except to his Maker."

They left the café, cautiously heading into the street. Like Nate, they weren't going to be taking any chances. Other men were coming out of various locations.

Red saw Doc Eli checking over those men lying on the

ground. A couple sat up holding some part of their body. He was glad to see the cowboy from Hawk's Wing was one of them. He was injured, but it didn't look life-threatening.

"Come on ya rascal," Nugget Nate was hauling a skinny youth up the middle of the street. "Here be the one I done found back there. Deputy Dak's with the one I knocked calliwampus. He ain't on his feet jest yet."

The men gathered in the middle of the street. Red was gratified that all the members of the posse were there. All were standing at least. Ben had a bullet hole in the crown of his hat. Jeb looked like he'd taken a glancing shot on the side of his leg.

Newt began asking questions, getting the stories from each of the men. Red, who was standing behind Massot, stepped out when the sheriff asked him a direct question. Newt's eyes got big. "Eli," he called. "We need you here. Red took a bullet."

All the men focused on Red. "It's fine. I think it went all the way through. It was pretty close range."

By now, Eli was at his side. "Well, you're a mess but going to be all right. Here's the exit hole. How about we go to my office and get that cleaned up? Yours seems to be the worst of the injuries I haven't treated yet. God favored us, that's for sure."

"Yeah, a bunch of dead outlaws and only some minor injuries for our side," Newt said. He began instructing the men to gather the bodies.

Massot tapped Red on his uninjured shoulder. "I'll go to Ben's store and get you a new shirt. Don't think Gema will want to see you in this one."

A commotion near the bank had everyone turning, hands poised to pull firearms from holsters. Dak was dragging a struggling man up the street. This outlaw was older than most of the men lying dead around town.

Noah Preston broke away from the group crowded around Newt. As always, he was dressed in black. His black duster hooked behind the holsters tied down on his legs. Tall and lean, he looked more like a gunslinger than a preacher.

With long strides, he closed the distance between himself and the outlaw. All three men stopped. Noah looked long at the man. Then, the preacher raised a fist and slammed it into his face, knocking the man to the ground, blood spurting out from his nose.

"That's for Chloe and all the other women and children you've abused throughout the years." Noah turned on his heel and walked back to the group. The steel grim expression on his face revealed he'd taken no pleasure in the action.

Silence reigned for a lengthy moment.

"As a pastor, are you supposed to do that?" Red couldn't keep himself from asking.

Noah shot him a cool glance. "I'll ask forgiveness later."

~~~~~

The silence was deafening once the shooting stopped. Gema, Laura, and the boys were still under the bed. Hank had stuck his head in the room shortly after the shooting began, yelling for them to stay hidden. Gema had grasped Laura's shoulder when she began squirming to scoot out.

"No, stay. No distract Hank. He want you safe."

Laura stilled and began reciting the Lord's prayer. They alternated between that and the twenty-third Psalm, her boys, cradled between Gema and Laura, joining in with the parts they knew. The women held tightly to each other's hand.

It seemed an eternity before the shots coming at the house, and the return fire died away. The gunfire coming from Main Street lasted longer.

"Can we get out, Mama?" Eddie asked.

"We'll wait on Hank."

Gema prayed he would come. That he was able to come. That the outlaws hadn't taken over the House. They didn't know who'd won the battle.

Bootsteps sounded, running in the hall. Laura tightened her grip on Gema's hand. Someone entered the room. The dimness left as the bedspread was lifted. All four hiding there gasped in a terrified breath.

"Come on out. We've won," Hank said, squatting down to peer under. Laura rolled over, releasing her son. Hank pulled her out as she burst into tears. He held her close for a moment before releasing her to help the others from the hiding place. Each one received a comforting hug.

"Red?" Gema asked, the name barely escaped her tight throat.

"I don't know anything about anyone. I know Hawk was okay when he signaled the outlaws attacking the House were all taken care of." When Gema started to run out, he grabbed her arm. "No, you stay here until someone comes to let us know it's truly all over. I'm not letting any of you off these floors until we get word from Newt."

Gema paced the hallway. She had to dodge as several of the other Ladies were doing the same thing; Myra, Newt's wife; Chloe, McIlroy's wife, and Cora, who was Dak's. Libby and Ruth were trying to quiet the eighteen-month-old twins. Boone and Mae sat in the corner holding each other. Their eyes were wide and filled with fear. Sally sat on a bed in the large bedroom several of the boys slept in. She had Nina on her lap and stared at nothing. Flora, holding Tadpole, sat on another with Ada leaning against her. The other children were sitting or standing out of the way of the pacing women.

Four went downstairs with Blanche who wanted to heat the stove so the food could be baked.

Hank set Duncan Ashburn, Chloe's son, to watch the alley. Dunc had wanted to be part of the men defending the house but, at only fourteen, Hank hadn't allowed it. Being assigned the task now that the shooting seemed to be over mollified the boy's wounded pride.

"Yo, the House."

Everyone stilled. Hank eased the revolver from his holster and entered a bedroom on the front side of the building.

"Who calls?" he yelled.

"It be McIlroy. Sheriff sent me. It's safe. The gang's either dead or in custody."

Chloe, carrying Lil-Pen, was running down the stairs. Dunc abandoned his position and followed on her heels. Myra and Cora crowded in next to Hank to look out the window.

"Newt and Dak are fine," McIlroy called.

Gema waited for him to say Red was, too. He didn't. Maybe she should go ask. She couldn't make her feet move. Fear that he was dead had blood pounding in her ears.

Women and children streamed passed her, heading downstairs. Still, Gema couldn't make her feet take any steps. Myra grabbed her hand as she headed to the stairs.

"Come on. Ya won't learn anything standin' here." She pulled Gema along behind her.

Hawk was talking to Blanche as they reached the bottom of the stairs. He came to Gema and grabbed her shoulders. She nearly collapsed.

"He's going to be fine. He took a shot in the shoulder. Doc Eli's tending to him now."

Gema jerked away and burst out the door. Picking up her skirts, she jumped off the end of the porch, ran up the street and across to the medical office. Jeb was sitting in a chair in the waiting room, a bandana tied around his thigh.

"Red?" she asked.

"First room." Jeb pointed.

"You well?"

"Right as rain."

Gema didn't bother to knock. She just opened the door and rushed in. Doc Eli and Red looked at her as she stilled in the doorway. Eli was wrapping a bandage around the injured shoulder while Red sat on the table.

"Let me tie this off, and he's all yours, Gema."

She barely heard him. Her eyes darted from Red's shoulder to his face and back.

"There." Eli pulled the knot tight. "I'll tend Jeb in the

other room. You take all the time you need." Eli gave Gema a quick hug as he left the room, shutting the door as he went.

Red gave her a sheepish grin and held out his uninjured arm. She flew to him and began sobbing. "It's all right, honey. I'll be good as new in a few days."

Gema just kept crying. She wrapped her arms around him and held on with fierce determination, burying her face against his neck.

"Honey, I need to breathe," Red whispered in her ear.

She loosened her hold but didn't release him. She couldn't. All she could think of was that Red had been shot. He could have been killed, and he'd never know how much she loved him.

~~~~~

Gema pulled back and studied Red's face again. "You okay. Real okay?"

"Yes, honey. I'm fine. You?"

"I well. Much scared. Laura, boys, me. We hide under bed. Prayer much." She knew her English wasn't good at the moment. She could only make simple sentences. All she wanted to tell him flowed through her head in Russian. The words he could understand stuck in her throat.

Taking his face between her hands, she kissed him. Long and hard. Then, she looked at him and kissed him again. And again.

When her fear and worry subsided, Gema leaned against his intact shoulder and tucked her head against his neck. "I love you. So scared you die in gunfight. Never have chance to say words."

Red's hand, which had been stroking her hair, stilled. He pulled back and tipped her head up with his fingers. His steel gray eyes searched her face. "Oh, honey. I love you, too. I was afraid of the same thing. That I'd be killed in the battle and never be able to tell you how much I love you."

Red kept his fingers under her chin and lowered his lips to hers. The kiss was soft and long.

Neither heard the door open. A throat cleared, causing them to break apart.

"Sorry," a red-faced Massot said. "Um, I brought you a new shirt." He leaned over and set the parcel on a chair. Backing out, he shut the door, leaving Gema and Red alone again.

Red took advantage of the moment and lowered his head again.

~~~~~

The after-effects of the shootout left all those involved exhausted. It was late in the day, so Hawk announced to his men that they could stay in town that night. He'd pay for hotel rooms. Sure they'd have to share, and a couple of the rooms had shot out windows, but the treat of a night in a real hotel wasn't something to be refused.

With the café shot up, the meal the Ladies had fixed was eaten in the dining room at the house. The men who had never stepped foot in the place looked around the room with interest. Nate offered to bring a couple of jugs of his squeezin's, but the offer had been politely declined by Blanche.

Gema fluttered around Red, making sure he was comfortable and doing the opposite. Finally, he pulled her onto his lap and wrapped his arm around her. "I'm fine, honey. You're making me nervous with all your flitting. You just sit right here and let the Ladies serve the meal."

"But I should help."

"Well," he laughed. "You weren't helping, with your attention focused on me, so just stay here." He hugged her close and gave her a quick peck on the cheek.

While everyone enjoyed dessert, Nate stood up. "Pastor Noah done thanked the Lord fer the endin' of the King Gang. He done it in a right 'n proper way, too. This here Saturday night, I'm a gonna host a shindig ta thank all them what helped in bringin' the varnmints evil ways ta a close. The whole town an' all the ranches an' such around 'll be invited. My Penny'll play some on her fiddle." A glance at Penny's face had him changing the last sentence. "'Scue me, on her violin. Then, the hoedown'll commence. Seems we be a needin' some culturation."

While Nate went on talking, Gema clutched Penny's arm. They were seated next to each other.

"You have violin? You have music?"

"Yes," Penny said. "Do you play?"

"I no have violin anymore. Papa sold, but have some music papers." Gema could hardly contain her excitement. "If I get paper, I copy music? Would like to have more. Jeb let me play his violin."

"Of course, my dear. Actually, I'll give you whatever I have duplicates of. I'll sort them tomorrow, and when you come to town on Saturday, I'll give them to you."

Red, sitting beside Gema, leaned toward them. "If you ladies would excuse me for a moment. I want to go check on Ralph and Blackie. Gema, please stay here until I come get you. I don't want you walking to the hotel by yourself. I won't be long."

"Don't worry, Mr. Dickerson. Your wife and I have a lot to talk about now that we know we have something in common." Penny smiled at Red and Gema.

Red touched Gema's cheek and left, Jeb went with him.

~~~~~

Red left Jeb at the hotel. He'd stopped by there after they checked on the horses at the livery and made one other stop. Jeb's grin and slap to Red's back was a mixed blessing since he'd smacked the wounded shoulder.

"You done a good thing there, Red. Gema's going to be loving on you for a long time."

Red didn't comment. That wasn't why he'd done it, but he'd certainly take any loving she wanted to give him. Maybe not tonight since his shoulder was throbbing badly. That didn't dim his smile as he went to the House to pick up his wife.

He still couldn't believe she loved him. She was such a beautiful young woman. He'd felt so guilty that they'd had to marry. She could have had the pick of any of the younger men of the area. He'd tried so hard to show her that he valued and honored her as his wife.

Still, he'd felt inadequate since, not only had they been obligated to get married, but he was so much older than her. He knew, in his head, that was often the case on the prairie and in the West, but it hadn't been their choice. Even when couples with an age difference chose to marry for convenience, they did choose. Gema and he hadn't had the choice.

When she'd first said the words, Red hadn't believed they were anything other than her fear for him speaking. Then she'd kissed him, and he knew. They'd kissed before. Many times since Gema's session chopping wood. But that kiss was different. More. It told him of her love. Made him believe her words.

He only hoped she believed his.

When he'd realized his feelings that morning as he ran up the stairs to get her, he couldn't take the time to think about them. He'd had to get her to town and ride out with the posse. Red had held her closer to him as they rode to town than he ever had before.

Red grinned as he crossed the street. He didn't think he'd ever teach her to ride a horse. Having her sitting in front of him in the saddle was one of the joys of his life. The first time they'd ridden that way was to shelter her as much as he could from the storm. After they married and he found out she didn't know how, there never seemed to be time to begin teaching her. Now, he didn't want to. He liked being able to hold her close as they rode.

Red took the steps to the porch two at a time and knocked on the front door. Gema answered with a huge smile on her face. "Come. We say goodbye and thank you."

As they walked to the hotel, Gema asked, "Can we come early to town for party? Mrs. Penny want to give me music. Maybe let me play her violin. Much better than Jeb's, I think."

Red squeezed her hand. "I'm sure you're right. I'll ask

Hawk. I'm sure he'll give me permission."

When they were in their hotel room, Gema began unbuttoning her bodice. Red stopped her. "Wait. I have something for you. I ordered it quite a while back. It just came in." He got the parcel from under the bed, where he'd hidden it.

Gema sat on the bed and unwrapped it with shaking hands. The shape gave her a clue as to what it was. When she opened the latches and lifted the lid, she gasped.

"Oh, Red. Oh, Red." Tear-filled eyes looked up at him. "It's beautiful."

Red cupped her cheek with his hand. "Not as beautiful as you. I ordered this as soon as I came to town, after that first time you played Jeb's violin. You played so beautifully even after so long not being able to practice. I knew you had to have one."

Gema set the violin case on the bed and stood, reaching for him to hug. "If I not love you already, I sure to love you now. Thank you."

Red captured her lips with his. When he finally broke the kiss, he said, "I wanted to give you back the music that is in your heart even before I knew I loved you. I'm so glad I did. So glad I'm the one who found you in the woods that day. I love you and am so glad you love me."

Gema gave him a teasing grin. "I'm glad for all that, too. Love my old geezer very much."

EPILOGUE

NUGGET NATE Ryder watched as his beloved Penny and Gema Dickerson played some classical duet on their violins. Penny had announced the name of it before they'd begun, but he couldn't make hide nor tail of what the words meant. Didn't matter. Penny was happy. That's all that mattered to him.

The morning after the shootout, Gema and Red had shown up at the Pullman. Gema was beaming with delight, the new violin case in her hand. She and Penny had disappeared into the rail car and spent several hours sorting music and playing tunes.

The day after the shootout, Nate and Red had spent the time discussing the events of the day before, as well as more incidents the King Gang had perpetrated over the years. Then, Nate had eyed Red. "I reckon you'll do, Red. Weren't sure after what I heard 'bout you an' Laura Duffle."

Red turned the color of his name. "I know I messed that up. I think God had a hand in it all. He had other plans for me and for Laura and Hank. Better plans. Hank's been my best friend for years. Did you know that?"

"Cain't say 'at I did."

"We're still best friends." Red explained that Hank was

the first person he thought of when he wanted someone to protect Gema.

"Mighty good friends like that is hard ta come by. You's blessed ta have one."

"I know. Now, I need to get my wife and get back to Hawk's Wing. We'll see you Saturday."

Red came to stand by Nate, bringing his thoughts back to the party. "They sound real nice playing together, don't they. I know Gema was excited to play with Penny. She practiced everyday. I had to stop her from making her fingers bleed pressing the strings."

"I'm sure you thought of other ways to occupy her." Nate's grin was wide. He watched Red blush, then stifled a laugh. He didn't want to disturb the violinists.

After the women took their bows, they struck up a lively dance tune, and other men and women began playing instruments.

Nate watched the Ladies who'd come to Stones Creek from Sanctuary Place in Iowa. There were still three unmarried Ladies living in the House. There were the women from the King Gang as well as the children. He was considering what to do with them. The women weren't ready to be considered. They needed time at the Place to heal from their traumatic pasts. They needed to know the love of God, as well as learn how to survive in society. The children needed the same. The boys might need a stronger hand than what was available at the Place. He'd think on that.

Nate glanced up at the ceiling of the warehouse his shindig was being held in. "I got's me a feelin' I ain't supposed to be aheadin' out o' Stones Creek jest yet."

He looked around the room. There was Blanche. He'd seen how Hawk looked at her.

Libby had the twins dancing as she held their hands. Nate glanced at the new lawyer in town, the one with the high faluntin' name. He was sure glad the townsfolk had started calling him Four.

Nate wanted to talk with Massot, the carpenter. He followed the man's gaze. The focus was on Ruth Naylor.

Something ran up Nate's spine. Yep, tweren't time fer he an' Penny to leave town jest yet. He had a couple of inclinings about how things might turn out, but wouldn't do anything to move them along until he'd gotten a better message from the Lord. Nate had run ahead of God a few times in the past, and he'd learned. He wasn't going to do that now.

The tall mountain man strode across to the stage. "Come on, Penny, m'love. Come an' takes a turn around the floor with me," Nate called. Penny smiled, set her violin carefully on a table, and walked to the edge. Nate swung her down, kissing her soundly.

Red followed his lead, and soon, Gema was in his arms as they danced to the music in his own heart.

A NOTE FROM SOPHIE

I hope you enjoyed **Music of Her Heart**. Please take a moment to leave a review on Amazon. For independently publishing authors like myself, the reviews are extremely valuable in getting our work noticed. <u>If you take just a few minutes you could help someone else find their next favorite book.</u>

Although Amazon says they require 20 words they will post it with fewer. You can pad your review with the title of the book and author name.

If you haven't read how Chloe Ashborn made the choice to go to Sanctuary Place, get the short story for free by signing up for Sophie's VIP newsletter.
        BookHip.com/ZZANRG

<u>BookHip.com/ZZANRG</u>

Thank you.

Sophie

P.S. Keep going to find the first chapter of the next book in the Stones Creek Ladies of Sanctuary House Series. It's Ruth and Massot's story titled **His Protective Wings**.

Sophie Dawson

BOOKS BY SOPHIE DAWSON

Cottonwood Series

Healing Love

Lord's Love

Giving Love

Redeeming Love (With George McVey)

Stones Creek Series

Leah's Peace

Chasing Norie

Chloe's Choice (Short Story)

Chloe's Sanctuary

Stones Creek Ladies Of Sanctuary House

Laundry Lady's Love

Love's Infestation

Mold and Marriage

Spots Before Marriage

Mice and Marriage

Java Cupid Multi-Author series

Java Priority

Java Protect

Single Books

Seeing The Life

Rescued By Love

If you enjoyed this book and would like to find other great Christian Indie Authors reads, follow the link below. Christian Books in Multiple Genres, Join Christian Indie Author ~ Readers Group on Facebook. Opportunities for free books and giveaways.

HIS PROTECTIVE WINGS
Chapter 1
Stones Creek, Colorado
November 1868

Ruth Naylor knew she was being watched. She could feel it. Had been aware of it for several weeks. The sensation sent chills up her spine. As much as she told herself it was nonsense to think some man was watching her, Ruth couldn't shake the feeling. With several of the Ladies who lived at Sanctuary House marrying and moving out, taking their children with them, her child care duties were reduced. That meant she had to find a different source of income. That meant dealing with and going to meet with men.

Now, Ruth stood on the porch of Sanctuary House and looked across the street at the carpenter shop. Arty Massot, the growly man who built most of the buildings in Stones Creek, had approached her last Sunday after worship service and said he'd heard she was looking for cleaning jobs. It was true, she was. The thought of going into a man's living quarters to clean tied her stomach in knots. It also seemed to have nailed her boots to the floor boards of the porch. But she needed the job.

Ruth pried her feet from the where they seemed to be fastened and descended the steps. With determination, she walked across the street, to the door of the carpentry shop. Should she knock, or go right in? It was a place of business after all. Lifting her hand, Ruth forced herself to turn the knob and open the door.

The smell of sawdust was thick in Ruth's nostrils. Every surface including the floor had a covering of the stuff. There were partially completed projects around the room with plenty of space to work on each one. Massot was sanding the top of a table, his back toward her.

Ruth studied the piece he was working on. It was unusual. Rather than a rectangle, square or circle, the table's edges were irregular. She realized the top was made from a cross section cut from the trunk of a huge tree. The concentric circles of the growth rings creating a beautiful design on its surface. To have dried the wood in such a way that it didn't split from the edge to the center spoke of the skill and knowledge of the carpenter polishing the table with such care.

Several other pieces of furniture were unusual, also. There were two small end-tables made in a similar fashion as the large one with a cross section cut as the top. The legs were made of wood bent in 'U'-shapes. Two partially assembled chairs were being built in the same manner; the frame made from trunks or branches of trees.

Massot turned around and jerked, startled to see Ruth standing just inside the door. "Oh, Miss Naylor, forgive me. I didn't realize you had come in. I get lost in my work." His low raspy voice sent shivers down Ruth's spine, doing strange things to her middle.

"I'm sorry. Should I have knocked?" Ruth twisted her fingers together.

Massot stepped forward. "No, of course not. This is a place of business. Anyone can come right in during business hours."

Ruth nodded. "I— um, you— um, mentioned you were looking for someone to clean your living quarters. She glanced around the messy workspace. It could use a good cleaning too, though she would never say so.

He must have noticed her perusal. "I know. This place is filthy also. I've been very busy building houses and furniture. There hasn't been time to shovel it out." He gave a slight kick to the thick layer of sawdust trampled on the floor.

Ruth didn't know what to say, so she said nothing, waiting for him to speak.

"Come, I'll show you what I'd like you to clean." He moved to the staircase along the back wall. She was surprised, since there was an exterior one on the side of the building, also. Not many had both.

Following him up the steps, Ruth found both sets shared the same landing. Massot opened the door and entered his living area. He cleared his throat. "As you can see, I'm in desperate need of help."

That was an understatement. The room they entered was a parlor of sorts. Or maybe it was more nearly correct to say the space they entered was the parlor. It appeared the entire upstairs of the building was one large open space with a sitting area or parlor near the stairs. To the far right were stacks of lumber seemingly sorted by type of wood and sizes of boards.

Behind the seating space was a large cookstove, cabinets, and a small table with two chairs. Further on, along the front of the building was a bed, dresser, and washstand. The only completely walled section was directly behind the stove. Stud walls divided the other areas. It was as if he'd stopped working on the apartment before doing the lath and plaster to complete the walls.

Plus the place was a mess. Sawdust was tracked everywhere. It also covered most surfaces. Brown paper, articles of clothing, books, newspapers, tools, rolls of paper she thought might be blueprints were scattered all over. The windows were covered with sawdust and grime, as were the exterior walls.

The room was surprisingly warm for such a large open space. Ruth wondered how that could be but didn't ask. Massot had told her, the previous Sunday when he'd asked if she would be willing to clean his apartment, that it was a disaster and he didn't know where to start. Ruth barely did herself.

"Mrs. Naylor, as you can see, I'm in desperate need of someone to make order out of this chaos and to keep it up. I'm sick of living in such a mess but don't have the time, knowledge, or inclination to do the work it will take to do so. I'm willing to pay well for you to do the initial cleaning and then pay a fair wage for your continued services." The amount he offered wiped away the doubts she had of working in the man's home. Or at least she was willing to

Music of Her Heart

put them aside until he broke what little trust she had in any man.

"Yes, this place could stand for a strong wind to blow through to get most of the evidence of your job sent out the window. Since it's the end of November, that's not possible. I don't think opening the windows is such a good idea in this cold weather."

"Then, you'll take the project on?" Massot's hopeful tone almost brought a smile to Ruth's lips.

"Where will you be while I clean?" she asked.

"Not up here. I'll either be working downstairs or on a house here in town. With winter coming, I'll be here more often than in the warmer weather. I won't come up when you are here, so long as you let me know when you arrive. I'd appreciate you telling me when you finish, also."

"Since you'll pay me when I leave, I most certainly will tell you when I leave as well as when I come."

Massot grinned at her. "Thank you. Do you want to start today?"

"I'll need to go back to the house and change into my work clothes."

"Thank you Miss Naylor. You are a Godsend. I was about ready to chuck everything out the window and start over."

Ruth descended the exterior staircase, leaving Massot to go down the interior back to his shop. She'd heard that he was grumpy and growly from others living in and around Stones Creek, but she'd not seen that side of him. Anytime he spoke with her, Massot had been unfailingly polite. Now, she just needed to conquer her unease at being in the building while he was the only other person on the premises.

Ruth waked across to Sanctuary House willing her stomach to unclench. Men, especially the attentions of men, made Ruth extremely nervous. Twelve years ago, a prominent businessman had stalked Ruth for months. Being only seventeen and innocent, she hadn't been aware of it. One day, saying he had gotten in a special order he thought she might like, the man trapped her in the back room of his store. What occurred there, Ruth didn't want to think about. When she told her parents what had happened to her, they hadn't believed her. The rape left Ruth with child. She'd been kicked out of her family as a slut and a lier.

Ruth had walked to the next town carrying what little she could pack in a carpet bag and the few dollars she'd earned from selling eggs. Hoping to find some kind of work, Ruth had found something better.

A tall mountain man, dressed in dirty buckskins and his well-dressed, dignified wife seemed to have been waiting for her. As Ruth walked up Main Street, the man strode up to her and said, "I'm a believin' you's the gal we's a been waitin' fer, my Penny 'an me. I done had me a Callin' 'bout a young woman whose been dealt with mighty poorly. Since I don't rightly knowst why any lady as young as yer be should be a wanderin' inta town with only a carpet bag an' a sorrowful face, you be the one, I's sure. Penny, m'love. I done found her. Reckon we kin be a headin' ta Sanctuary Place now."

Ruth had just stared at him. How could he know she'd been unjustly accused and found guilty when she was the victim of a heinous act? She'd backed away, slowly. She'd heard about men who tried to lure women by promising them aid. Instead, they often ended up in brothels selling themselves, receiving only pennies while the brothel owner kept the majority of the fee charged.

It had taken Penny Ryder, beloved wife of the famous Nugget Nate Ryder, to convince Ruth the offer of help was genuine. After buying her a meal in the local café, the journey across Wisconsin had begun. They ended up in Iowa at the mission for women called Sanctuary Place that was sponsored by the couple. It was where Ruth's daughter, Kathryn, was born eleven years ago.

In July, eight Ladies had arrived in Stones Creek, Colorado. They'd come to Nugget Nate's new Sanctuary House to begin new lives and possibly find husbands in the women starved West. Ruth didn't necessarily want a husband, but the opportunity for a new start for herself and her daughter lured her to join the Ladies moving to Colorado.

The goal was for them to find husbands but each woman had to fine jobs to support themselves in the meantime. Ruth had been tending the children of the other Ladies living in Sanctuary House while they worked. With several now married and the older children in school, the number she cared for during the day had dwindled. Ruth now needed additional work to supplement her income.

Birdie Pullman, who had been doing cleaning for area businesses, had married a widower with three children within a week of meeting him back in September. Ruth had been offered the job of cleaning the general store owned by

Ben Cutler when he and his family moved into the house Massot was building for them. It would be finished shortly and the move would take place before Christmas. Sara, Ben's wife, had asked Ruth to begin cleaning now since she was in an interesting condition and not feeling well much of the time.

The cleaning jobs would have to be done after the Ladies whose children Ruth watched came home from their jobs. That meant she would be doing the cleaning on Saturdays or in the evenings. It wasn't ideal as Ruth didn't like the idea of being in the buildings alone at night. She wasn't pleased with the prospect of walking back to the House in the dark either. At the moment, it couldn't be helped. Massot wanting her to work on Saturdays eased those concerns, but having to be alone with him in the building brought others to mind.

~~~~~<<>>~~~~~